THE BOY NEXT DOOR

A STANDALONE ENEMIES-TO-LOVERS ROMANCE

NATASHA L. BLACK

COPYRIGHT

JAYSON

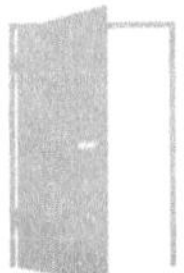

I cracked open a bottle of water and drained half of it while Mark talked about the next song on our setlist. Great guy and great singer, but every once in a while, I just wished he'd just start the damned song already. The adrenaline rushing through my veins made me impatient, and my hands twitched restlessly, itching to pick out the beat that would lead us into our next song.

It was hot in there that night, and the AC wasn't working hard enough to combat it. Someone had opened the doors to let a little fresh air in, and I knew as we finally launched into the next riff that our music must be echoing out into the night. Occasionally, people would pause to peer inside. Usually, they would then drift in, heads already bobbing to the beat.

That only stoked my excitement further. We hadn't made it, not yet, but our fan base was growing every day, and they were starting to sing along with our more popular songs.

What a rush to know that we could affect people like that.

We finished the set with a bang, and the applause was deafening. I was grinning ear to ear as I put my sticks lovingly into their bag and stood up. Luke, the bassist, nodded at me, an equally large smile on his face. He clearly felt just as exhilarated as I did.

Mark didn't look at either of us; he only had eyes for the group of ladies who had stayed near the front, dancing through the whole show. A couple of them had come out to our shows before; others were new. Mark barely had to try to charm them. In the next second, he had his arm around one and was winking at another, while a third pressed a drink into his hand. I shook my head.

Luke came over to me, clearly ignoring Mark's antics as he always did. "Man, we were *on fire* tonight!" he said.

I laughed and bumped my fist against his. "Yeah, that solo you pulled was awesome!"

Luke looked critically around. The best part was, even though we had finished our set, people were sticking around. That meant that the venue would be pleased with us. We had brought people in, and we had got them buying drinks.

And a happy venue meant more gigs to come.

Not only that, but we had a pretty big crowd there that night. We were nearly at capacity, by the looks of it.

Which meant that soon, we would be able to start booking larger venues, bringing in an even bigger crowd. I didn't want to get too far ahead of myself, but it was starting to feel like it was only a matter of time before we started getting the right kind of notice.

Before we *made it*.

It was an incredible feeling. I'd spent the past few years

pouring everything I had into this band. Blood, sweat, tears, and then some. I had poured my heart out into the lyrics; I had practiced drum solos until my hands were raw and my callouses had callouses. Any money that I had, I spent on things for the band, knowing that eventually, if I gave it my all, it would pay off.

We had a shot at making it big. I was surer of it than ever before. Our big break was right around the corner.

My face fell as I saw Carter, our guitarist, over at the bar. He was well on his way toward shitfaced, and as I watched, he took another shot alongside a giggling girl while another girl egged them on. Between him and Mark, I didn't know who was worse.

I shook my head. While Luke and I seemed to be on the same page about pushing the band forward to that next level, it sometimes felt that Mark and Carter were doing whatever they could to hold us back and make sure that we were stuck playing in garages and dive bars for the rest of our lives.

I couldn't imagine the band without them. At the same time, I didn't know how things were going to work out going forward. I knew there was a particular lifestyle that came along with being a rock star, but at the end of the day, it was still a job. It was a serious business. You weren't going to get very far without putting in the work.

That was what Carter and Mark didn't seem to understand. We could party later, once we were on top. Once we'd released a hit album, once we'd really broken through. What they were doing now would only damage our reputation. If Mark got himself thrown out of another bar or Carter got in another fistfight for sleeping with the wrong girl, I was going to lose it.

Nights like these never ended at the bar, either. It

wasn't just that after a show, they went out and had some fun, enjoying the perks of our rising stardom. They seemed to think that it was okay to be late to practices the next day, or to show up still drunk, reeking of booze and sex.

We hadn't written any new material in ages because they couldn't seem to hold it together for long enough for us to hammer out a chorus, or even to rehearse consistently. Either they were taking advantage of the free drinks that everyone bought them after a show, grinning and charming everyone in the vicinity, or else they were down in the dumps and drowning their sorrows in booze, wondering why we hadn't made it yet.

It was killing me. If we were going to make it big-time, we were going to have to actually pull it together and work, and I was starting to worry that maybe the two of them didn't have it in them.

I shook my head, trying not to dwell on it tonight. I was only going to depress myself when what I really wanted was to revel in the night that we'd had. I started grabbing our equipment, in part to give me something to do with my hands and in part because I didn't want anyone to spill anything on it or get the bright idea that this was karaoke night and that they were welcome to bash on our gear.

I was just putting the last of the cases in the van when Trixie came up to me, grinning. "Hey, you," she said. "Have you let anyone buy you a drink yet?"

I shrugged. "Nah," I said simply. Trixie was one of our most notorious groupies, coming out to nearly every one of our shows and commenting all over our social media. While it was nice to have someone who was apparently so incredibly interested in everything that we did, I couldn't help but wonder if she was in it for all the wrong reasons. Either she wanted to say that she'd been the one to "discover" us before we were big, or she just wanted to sleep with one or all of us.

I wasn't sure which it was, but I wasn't sure that I really cared.

The truth was, she was cute. Without a doubt. She had brown hair that had been cut short in the back, longer in the front, and styled messily. She had a kind of punk edge to her styling, but I'd never seen her in anything that wasn't form-flattering and sexy at the same time.

She flirted with me after nearly every show, and it would be only too easy to bring her home with me, bang her senseless, and then send her off home. No strings and no expectations. The rock-and-roll lifestyle.

But I wasn't feeling it tonight. Not that I ever really was. I rarely brought anyone home with me, no matter how many girls showed interest in me, no matter how cute or attractive they were. I was too busy trying to build the band and, I guess, show a good example to Mark and Carter.

Besides, I had a hard time sharing a bed with people; I never seemed to sleep that well. At the same time, I didn't want to be the asshole who mandated that a girl leave imme-diately afterward. It just wasn't worth the hassle to sleep with anyone.

So as Trixie grinned at me, I slowly shook my head. "Not tonight, Trixie. I'm sorry," I said.

She looked disappointed but resigned. "Yeah, fine," she said, rolling her eyes. She darted in to kiss me lightly on the cheek, though. "I'll see you next time," she said. As she walked away, she turned back to me, walking backward, somehow managing not to trip in her sky-high heels. "By the way, you were amazing tonight."

I laughed. "Thanks," I said honestly. She might follow our bands for all the wrong reasons, but at the end of the day, she had been a fan for a while now. Praise from her meant that I really had done a great job that night. That something had been different from last time, that we were getting *better*.

At least, I liked to think so, anyway.

I headed inside to gather up the rest of my bandmates, or at least say my goodbyes. I had a feeling that yet again, Mark and Carter were going to refuse to come home in the van. Sure enough, I was right. I was seething when I got back in the driver's seat. Luke slipped silently into the passenger's side, clearly sensing my mood, or maybe feeling the same way himself.

This was starting to get old. I couldn't imagine the band as anything other than the four of us, but maybe it was time for a change.

Except that a change could kill the whole band's momentum. Besides, I knew that part of why we drew the crowds that we did was because our singer and our guitarist were both good-looking and charming. We wouldn't have the same sex appeal without them.

I didn't know what to do, and as I lay in my bed a little while later, I couldn't help but feel restless and dissatisfied, no matter how well the show had gone earlier in the night.

I dragged myself over to my drum set. The one set up in the corner of my disorderly but clean one-bedroom apartment wasn't quite as tricked out as the one that I used for gigs, but it was good to practice on all the same.

I had been lucky to find this place. It was one side of a duplex unit, but I didn't have to worry about the noise because my next-door neighbor, Mr. Lake, was almost entirely deaf. He never complained, and I could bang out my frustrations until I was able to relax again.

Except that tonight, I was just getting started when I

suddenly noticed a banging at my front door. I frowned, sticks stilling in the middle of the beat for a new song that I had been hoping to work on for a couple of weeks now.

I slowly stood up, wondering who could be there at that hour. Maybe one of my bandmates?

I pulled open the door to find a stranger standing there, though, dressed in a green silk robe and glasses, her arms crossed over her ample chest and an angry expression on her face. Her red hair escaped out of the bun that she had tried to pull it into, and it was a furious electricity that animated her.

"Do you have any idea what time it is?" she snapped.

I glanced at my watch, belatedly realizing that I wasn't wearing it.

I shrugged. "Late, I guess."

The woman narrowed her eyes at me. "Late, I guess," she mimicked, clearly not impressed. "It's after midnight, and I need to work tomorrow, so stop banging on your damn drums!"

I blinked at her. As pissed as she clearly was, I couldn't help but notice how cute she was too. I felt a stirring of interest in my groin. It would be so easy for me to pull her inside, to open her robe, to suck kisses along her skin...

Except I didn't even know who she was or what she was doing there on my doorstep. Besides, she had interrupted my drum practice, and the only way that I was going to make it with the band was if I kept practicing hard like I had been. I couldn't deal with interruptions like this. No matter how cute they were.

"I don't know who you think you are, but you can't just come over here and demand that I quit playing," I said, jutting out my lower lip.

She stared at me incredulously. "What, would you

rather me call the police?" she asked finally. "I thought I was doing the nice thing by giving you a warning before I did that, but I can call them now if you'd like. I was just trying to be *neighborly*." She spat out the word like she thought I was being anything but.

"Neighborly?" I asked blankly. What the hell was she talking about? I had never seen her before. I frowned, trying to figure out what to say next. Finally, I found my voice.

"Who *are* you?"

2

———————

LEAH

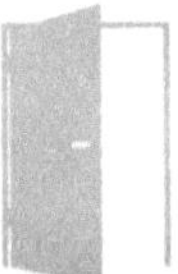

I wasn't sure that I had ever been this pissed before. Apartment-living situations always had their draw-backs, but after viewing a string of terrible places there in Los Angeles, I had thought that I had finally found the perfect place. It was a one-bedroom, so I didn't have to worry about roommates who were unclean, unfriendly, or otherwise unfortunate people to share a place with.

I had been skeptical about the proximity to my neighbor from the very start. The duplexes on this street were relatively well spaced out, enough so that my neighbors on the one side didn't bother me. But what about the person on the other side of the walls from me?

The landlord had sworn up and down that he had never received any complaints from his previous tenant about the person living next door. Well, that tenant must have been a fan of loud banging all night long, because that was all that I had heard for the last half hour now, and it was driving me crazy.

I mean, seriously, what kind of person living in such close proximity to his neighbors like this thought that it was okay to make so much noise at all hours of the night? Some asshole wannabe rock star, apparently. Welcome to LA.

And now he was acting like he had done nothing wrong.

"I have to work tomorrow," I said, emphasizing the word "work" as though maybe he hadn't heard it before. I hadn't moved to LA for a new job just to be kept up all night the day before I started said job. I didn't want to start things off on the wrong foot with my new neighbor, but seriously, what did he want me to do? I had tried putting in earplugs, and I had tried covering my head with my pillow, but nothing had worked. It was after midnight now. Enough was enough.

That said, I had to admit that my new neighbor was more than I had bargained for. I didn't know what I had expected—I guess just some older, washed-up rock star with no life. Maybe some guy who was so drugged up or wasted that he didn't even know what time it was.

He seemed sober, though. Moreover, he was hot, a lot hotter than I could have expected. He had jet-black hair that was just a bit sweaty, just enough that it stood up in spikes as though he had run a hand back through it while he was on his way to answer the door. He had piercing blue eyes, and when he folded his arms across his chest, no doubt in response to my own posture, I couldn't help but notice the tattoos that spiraled along his skin.

He was wearing a T-shirt and sweats, but I could only imagine from the breadth of his shoulders that he must be in good shape. *I suppose a drummer would have to be,* I thought.

Not that I was giving him any passes for keeping me up all night.

"I'm trying to work right now," he said, arching an eyebrow at me, a challenge on his face. "Anyway, I pay to live here. Mr. Lake doesn't care if I make noise, so I hardly see how it's any of your concern."

I threw my hands in the air. "It's my concern because I pay to live here too!" I snapped. "And who the hell is Mr. Lake?"

I didn't miss the way the drummer's eyes darted down to my cleavage, where my robe had come open. I huffed and closed it. *Boys.*

"Mr. Lake is my neighbor," the man said as though I hadn't just caught him leering at me. "He lives over there."

"No, *I* live over there," I said, connecting the dots. "I don't know what happened to the last tenant, but I live there now, and I don't appreciate the noise. So knock it off." With that, I turned on my heel and marched back to my apartment.

Let him start drumming again. I wasn't kidding when I said that I would call the police to file a noise complaint.

He didn't start back up, though. It was finally quiet. Something still kept me from sleeping, though.

It was partly that I was nervous about my big day tomorrow. It was such a leap of faith, moving to LA from my small hometown in Illinois. There was something about my new neighbor that reminded me that I didn't belong here. I wasn't trying to be a movie star or a musician or anything like that, but I had moved here to work for a big entertainment company.

Granted, I'd be an accountant. That was something that I was good at. I had proven myself in a string of internships while I was in college, and I knew that I had found what I was good at. What's more, I was excited for the company that I'd be working for. I knew that I would have the chance to excel at my job, and I had a feeling that I might have the chance to move up in the company chain.

Still, all of that didn't mean I wasn't worried that I might have made the wrong choice. I didn't know anyone here, and life was so different from life back in my quiet Midwestern town.

It's a good thing I don't scare easily, I thought.

I'd just have to take things one step at a time. The job wouldn't be that scary once I started it. I knew that. And living in LA wouldn't be as stressful once I made some friends.

My thoughts drifted back from work to the handsome drummer who lived next door. His drumming, while obnoxious for the hour, had been pretty decent. The guy probably knew the music scene pretty well. I wouldn't mind getting to know him better. Maybe I could get him to show me around.

I grimaced and rolled over, as though rolling over could shield me from those thoughts. Instead, my train of thought continued: I had probably ruined my chances of getting to know the guy any better with everything tonight.

For a moment, I felt a flash of guilt and disappointment. This wasn't the way that I wanted my LA chapter to begin. I didn't want him to think I was some uptight hick with a stick up my ass. No going back now, though.

In any case, it wasn't like I needed to be distracted by rocker bad boys. I was there to further my career. When I did have the time to date, it wasn't going to be a man who stayed up all night banging on drums; it was going to be someone quiet and steadfast. Someone who wanted a family and someone who was dependable. Someone considerate, most of all.

I tried to forget about the hottie next door and get some sleep. I had a big day the next day, and that was the thing that I needed to focus on first and foremost. I could worry about the rest of it afterward.

Still, the silence suddenly seemed almost too loud. I rolled over again, pulling my pillow over my head as though I *wanted* it to be that quiet. Eventually, I drifted off to a night of restless sleep.

3

JAYSON

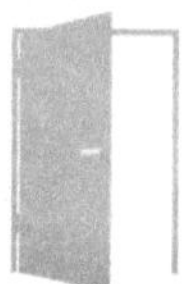

I gritted my teeth in frustration as I watched Mark flirt with the ladies he had brought with him, telling them some made-up story about how he had written the lyrics to the song that we were practicing. I tuned out the story, but I couldn't ignore what he was doing.

We were here in Luke's garage trying to rehearse. It was one of the few times we had all managed to be there nearly on time, and I had hoped we would rehearse a few things and then maybe get to work on something new. Finally.

Of course, as soon as I saw that Mark had brought companions, that idea went out the window. They were just here to watch, he had promised. But it was only a matter of time before he got distracted. As he always did.

We had been practicing here in Luke's garage for all the time we'd been a band. The house used to belong to his parents, until they had passed away suddenly in a freak car accident when he was just out of high school. It was the perfect space to rehearse in, somewhere far enough away from neighbors (and soundproof enough, anyway) that we didn't need to worry about interruptions.

Today, I couldn't seem to stop thinking about the fact that my place was no longer in the same class. I hadn't encountered my new neighbor in the few days since she had chewed me out for drumming late into the night. Nor had I played my drums late at night, though.

I wasn't caving to what she wanted. It wasn't that. I just had drummed it all out during the day.

That was what I was telling myself, anyway.

I was trying to focus on right now, though. This disastrous practice. It wasn't just Mark that was a problem. Carter was no better. He was either so hungover or so blitzed that he kept messing up his chords. Luke and I were the only people who were keeping a beat, and it was starting to piss me off.

"Can we get started already?" I finally snapped. "Look, I'll forget about working on anything new today because I can tell that's not going to happen, but we should at least rehearse 'Maggie Ann Says Goodbye' if we're going to play it at our next show."

Mark stared at me, his eyebrows rising. "Are you trying to tell me that we're not working?" he said. "We've already been through four of our songs and they've been fine. We know 'Maggie,'—I don't know why you're acting like we're suddenly not going to be able to play it. We wrote it."

I stared at him. There was a part of me that knew he was just trying to put on a show in front of the girls, but that didn't make it any better.

I exploded.

"Fine?" I shouted. "You think that the other songs have been fine? You forgot half the fucking lyrics of two of them, or made up stupid versions of your own, and neither you or

Carter were on beat. You're wasting our time dicking around when we need to work. There's a reason that we haven't debuted 'Maggie' yet. I don't think we're ready to play it in front of people."

"Oh, that's it?" Mark snarled. "You act like you're the only person in this band who has any say in it."

"I am, if I'm the one who wrote the song," I said flatly.

"You didn't write that song, not on your own," Mark said. "It belongs to all of us."

"Name one thing that you added to it," I said through gritted teeth, even though I knew that this wasn't what we needed to argue about. "And if you try to play it with the way that we've been sucking lately, you can do it without a drummer."

"The band isn't all about you," Mark said, rolling his eyes. "As for sucking, you could try playing on beat sometimes. That would help. Have you even been practicing lately?"

I nearly threw my sticks at him. But we were both interrupted by Carter, who suddenly went over to the fridge and grabbed a beer.

"Jesus Christ," I muttered, throwing my sticks down. "Everyone in this band had better pull their heads out of their asses if we're ever going to make it." I couldn't keep myself from storming out of there. We needed more practice, but clearly it wasn't going to happen now.

I headed back to my own house and sat down at my drum set in the corner. For a moment, I was too angry to play. Then, I started in on it, working out all of my frustrations.

The real trouble was that I couldn't imagine the band without Mark or Carter. As frustrating as they'd been lately, they were founding members. Mark's vocals were one of the things that we were known for. And Carter was a great guitarist when he wasn't out of his mind. Not only that, but we had all leaned on one another over the past few years. We had been through thick and thin together. The idea of bringing in someone new now was unimaginable.

Yet.

I just couldn't help thinking of the other possibilities. Could we find someone else to replace the two of them? Someone who could support Luke and me as we tried to capitalize on everything we had built so far, rather than dragging us down together as a team?

I slammed both of my sticks down on a cymbal crash. I didn't want to think about that.

Was it naive to think that the four of us who had made it this far could keep going? It definitely seemed crazy to think that we could cut out half of the members of the band and keep our momentum, but it wasn't like I could choose between Mark and Carter. I just wished they weren't making things so damn complicated.

There was a shadow outside. This late in the afternoon, all shadows were long, but this one was particularly so. My new neighbor, whatever her name was, walking past on the sidewalk, dressed in smart-casual work clothes. I paused in my drumming automatically.

Then, I scowled. I couldn't quit drumming every time I saw her come home. It was still early evening; it was my prerogative if I wanted to keep practicing. Maybe it would drive her crazy, but that was her problem. I hadn't had any trouble before she moved in.

And if I wasn't able to drum freely, I wasn't going to get any better. Or be able to cope with all the shit that was going on.

Still, there was a part of me that felt bad about it. She

had probably moved in there without any warning. Mr. Lake probably hadn't heard my drumming during his time there, so it had never been an issue before. She likely thought that she was moving into a quiet, somewhat residential area.

That wasn't my fault, but how she dealt with it wasn't going to become my problem, either.

I went over there and knocked on the door, waiting for her to appear. The moment she answered the door, she seemed to realize her mistake. She started to shut the door on me, but I was worked up from the thing with Mark earlier, and I needed one thing to go right today. If it was this, then fine.

"Listen here," I said before she could get a word in edgewise. "I've been living here for three years now, and I've always been able to drum whenever I wanted to. That's not going to change now. So I suggest you invest in a good pair of noise-canceling headphones or something and learn to deal with it."

I glared at her, but as she folded her arms across her chest again, I could see a speculative gleam of a challenge in her eyes. I had to admit, it turned me on a little to see that she wasn't going to be cowed.

"Learn to deal?" she scoffed. "Have you read your lease terms lately? I don't want to have to go to the landlord, but there are specific terms in there that stipulate the noise conditions. If you won't adhere to those and he won't do anything, well, I meant what I said the other night. I was just being nice because I just moved in here, but I'm not opposed to going to the police if I have to. I'm not going to put up with your shit. So I suggest that *you* find a way to deal, and maybe invest in some, I don't know, noise-canceling drums."

I stared dumbly at her. "Noise-canceling drums?" I finally snapped.

She shrugged. "I'm sure there's something out there so that people like you don't bug people like me in apartment complexes," she said, tossing her hair back. It was then that I realized that it was loose today. The curls were no more contained than they had been the other night, but there was something about the way they played along the creamy skin of her jaw...

I dragged my eyes back to hers, narrowing my gaze. I couldn't help the way that I was strangely attracted to her and her spunkiness, but I'll be damned if I was going to let her know that. I wouldn't let her have the upper hand.

"There's nothing in my contract about noise," I told her. "Anything that's in yours must have been added after I signed on. Which again was years ago."

She simply rolled her eyes, though. "Well, then I'll talk to the police about the city noise ordinance. Whatever I have to do," she insisted.

I stared at her. I couldn't help but feel vaguely taken aback. This woman had some balls. I couldn't help but feel admiration that she wasn't going to put up with my dick-head demeanor.

All the same, I knew that I couldn't give up. My career was at stake here. My freedom, my future, my release, everything.

Still, there was something about her that drew me in. I found myself wanting to get closer to her. So I did, crossing the gap between us. I leaned in, propping an arm against the door, hemming her in. "Where the hell did you come from, anyway?" I hardened my tone slightly. "Because around here, that's just not how we do things."

She stared up at me, her gaze stoic. Somehow, she didn't

seem even the slightest bit intimidated. "Where did I come from?" she echoed. "Out of your worst nightmares."

I blinked at her and then laughed, shaking my head. I couldn't help it. She was one of a kind.

Suddenly, the urge to kiss her struck me. The look on her face, though, told me that she would bite my lips off if I tried. I knew that we had accomplished everything that we would here and started to back out the door.

I turned back for one last look at her. Suddenly, with the light catching her in that way, burnishing her hair to a bright copper and making her green eyes look almost ethereal, winning the argument seemed a lot less important.

I stared at her, lost for words for a moment. Before I could gather my wits, she slammed the door shut in my face. I shook my head, but I was grinning as I walked away. My grin widened as she opened the door and shouted one last thing after me: "And the next time you push your way into my apartment like that, I'll tack on trespassing as well!"

I chuckled.

Things with my new neighbor were certainly going to be interesting. I knew that this feud wouldn't be enough to take my mind off my worries about the band, but it would at least be a welcome distraction.

4

LEAH

I looked around at the group as Piper excused herself to the restroom for a moment. I couldn't help but feel proud of myself. I might not be *friends* with most of the women who were scattered in our general vicinity, but I knew all of their names, and I didn't think that I had offended anyone too badly just yet.

This was the first girls' night out that I had been invited to with my new coworkers. Piper had invited me, and I took it that this was a weekly ritual. I was hoping that this would end that way for me as well.

I was so relieved that it was Piper who had been tapped to show me the ropes on my first day. She and I had become fast friends, and she had taken her duties beyond the office. She was funny, upbeat, and active, and she had offered to show me around LA as well as find me some friends. She had really taken me under her wing.

This was all still way out of my depth, but I had the

feeling that if I stuck around with Piper for long enough, maybe I would start to feel like I belonged here. Eventually.

When she had invited me to this girls' night, I guess I had expected something a little tamer. Maybe like the opportunity to get to know some of my new coworkers, maybe a karaoke night or pub trivia. Instead, we were at a crowded bar on Sunset Boulevard. The live music hadn't started yet, but I could already barely hear myself think.

It wasn't like we didn't have this kind of thing back home, or some variant of it. This was a Wednesday night, though. Apparently weekdays—and workdays—didn't seem to matter when you lived in LA. That was going to take some getting used to.

"You're going to love the band," one of Piper's friends said, leaning in toward me so that she could be heard. "They're really great. We've seen them a couple times before, and I think they could really explode."

One of the other girls laughed and draped her arm around the first girl's shoulders. "Ignore her. She only says that because she has the hots for the lead singer," she joked.

"I mean, can you blame me?" the other girl said, rolling her eyes and grinning.

I glanced toward the stage, hoping to catch a glimpse of this attractive singer. There was still no one there, though. I turned back to the group. It didn't matter, anyway. I wasn't interested in going home with someone that night. I wasn't interested in getting involved with rock stars in general.

And if I was interested, there's only one rock star I'd be getting with, I thought, my mind flitting back to my sexy, tattooed neighbor with the bad attitude. That wasn't going to happen, though. I was here for my career, and I was going to focus on that.

With that in mind, I turned to the girl next to me. "So, what department do you work in again?" I asked.

She groaned and put her hands over her ears. "You can't use that four-letter word on a girls' night out!" she proclaimed.

I blinked and looked around. The other girls were nodding in sage agreement. Megan's eyes twinkled as she leaned forward. "We haven't gone over the rules yet, but I'm not giving you a pass on that one," she said. "Anyone so much as mentions work while we're out at the bar, that means they have to buy a round of shots."

I made a face. Surely she wasn't serious, was she? I couldn't remember the last time I had done shots—maybe sometime in college? Weren't we all adults here? We all had to be in the office the next morning, and even though the anxieties of my first day on the job had somewhat worn off, I still didn't want to mess anything up.

But I didn't want to be the downer, or even more of the outsider than I already was. If this was the way they did things here in LA, then so be it.

Megan caught the bartender's arm and ordered a round of tequila shots to be put on my tab. I tried not to grimace at that as well. I could only imagine how much shots cost in a bar in LA, even if it was a bit of a dive. I could probably pay my rent for the cost of a round.

Note to self, do not talk about work with these people, I thought.

The shot burned as it went down, and I couldn't help but cough a little. I was used to having a couple of beers on a board game night, not doing shots with a group of girls who all let out a yell after they tipped one back.

I wasn't the last person to buy a round for us, either. It seemed like Megan came up with a new rule every other minute, but all the other girls were nodding along like this was normal. One shot became three, and soon I felt like I was blissfully floating in the clouds.

I could hear myself talking, and I knew that I was telling these virtual strangers way too much personal information—especially given the fact that they were my coworkers. Fortunately, just as I was starting to wonder if I should feel embarrassed, the band started playing, effectively shutting up any conversation that we might have had.

I cocked my head to the side as I listened, tapping out a beat with my foot. The girls were right—they were pretty good.

Everyone got up to dance, and Piper dragged me along with them. I frowned. Dancing wasn't usually my thing. Then again, tonight I was feeling the music, or at least the booze. I swayed with the rhythm, shaking my hips and bobbing with the beat.

I remembered what the girls had said about the singer being sexy, and I looked toward the stage. He was all right, I guessed, but you could definitely tell he *knew* that he was attractive. That had always been a turnoff for me. Guys like that were nothing but trouble.

My eyes slipped past him toward the drummer, who was pounding out the beat as though he were possessed by pure electricity. He happened to look at me at the same time that I looked at him. Or had he been watching me dance the whole time?

With a jolt, I realized that I knew him. Those dark blue eyes, those tattoos. It was none other than my new neighbor. And God did he look hot tonight, drumming his ass off.

My mind flashed back to that first night I had gone over there, when I had yelled at him to keep it down. I remembered the way he had stared when my robe slipped and he caught a glimpse of just the upper swell of my breasts. A similar heat went through me now, even as he dragged his gaze away and focused his attention back on his drums, launching into a particularly complex part of the song. I couldn't take my eyes off him, though. I was utterly mesmerized.

I found myself considering my neighbor in a new light. I had to admit, he was good. Like, really good. He wasn't just some wannabe rock star drumming away at midnight just to annoy me. He actually had something. If the pulsing bodies around me were anything to go by, I wasn't the only one to think so, either.

He was sexy as hell too. I wasn't the kind of girl to go chasing someone just because he was hot, but tonight, I almost wanted to. Maybe it was the liquor or the music or some combination of the two, but I suddenly wanted him.

Sure, he was nothing that I needed, but maybe it wouldn't hurt to see if he was as good with his hands when he wasn't drumming. I shivered with heat as I continued to gyrate, watching him closely without trying to seem too obvious about it. I wasn't sure who I'd be more embarrassed to have notice my sudden attention to him: the man himself or my coworkers.

I couldn't stop speculating over what it would be like to have him in bed with me, though. To have him strip me bare, to have him run his hands over my body. I didn't have a ton of experience with guys, and most of my sexual experiences had been vaguely disappointing.

I didn't think the drummer would disappoint, though. No, I had a feeling he could play my body as well as he could play those drums. For all the flash and passion that he poured into his playing, there was a certain tenderness as well, which was there in the way that he concentrated and the way he struck each beat.

I kept on dancing, my eyes on his, swaying seductively. Suddenly, I wanted to tease him. I wanted his eyes on me, wanting me as he played. I wanted to get inside his head, even if I never got the courage to go any further with him.

I couldn't help but feel disappointed as he kept his gaze trained on the instruments in front of him. He didn't look my way again, not even as the singer introduced their next song.

5

JAYSON

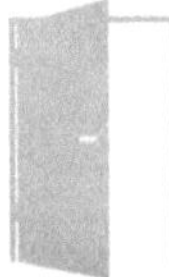

I couldn't believe she was there.

To be honest, when I first laid eyes on my new neighbor in the crowd, I had expected her to roll her eyes and storm out. Then I'd realized that she was dancing. And God, how she was dancing...

My cock was rock-hard from watching her. I'd tried my best to be surreptitious about it, peeking at her out of the corner of my eyes. The last thing I needed was for her to realize how much she got under my skin with her hips swaying to the beat.

What the hell was she doing there? Of all the places in LA, how had she just happened to come to our gig? I had to admit, I was revising my original opinion of her. When she had first shown up at my doorstep, yelling at me to keep quiet, I had decided she must be kind of a crazy cat lady trapped in a stunner's body.

Maybe that wasn't a fair assessment.

We finished the set, managing to make it through every

27

song more or less decently even though I knew that Carter was already well on his way to blitzed. We didn't add anything new, though, and I couldn't help wondering if things were starting to get stale for our groupies. Would they stop coming, eventually, when they realized we had nothing more to offer?

I couldn't think about that now, though. The only thing I seemed able to think about was my hot neighbor. I watched as she chatted with a group of girls near where she had been dancing before, a huge grin on her face. God, she was cute. She definitely looked like she had enjoyed herself. I wondered if that meant she would come out to more of our shows.

I found myself drawn toward her, like a magnet. I didn't know what I would say when I got to her, but I supposed I could reintroduce myself now that we weren't yelling at each other. I realized that I had never gotten her name.

Luke interrupted me, though. His eyes were shining with excitement. "Dude, I just looked at my phone," he said. "The venue owner, Jim, texted me while we were playing."

I grimaced. That could go either of two ways. We had done a decent job that night, but not our best. At this point, we couldn't afford to fuck things up. My eyes strayed to where Mark and Carter were at the bar. But then, my gaze was captured by a cheering group of girls doing shots—and wouldn't you know, but my new neighbor was right in the middle of them.

"He wants to book us for five more shows in the near future," Luke continued, dragging my attention back to him.

My jaw dropped. "Wow, really?" I couldn't help but feel shocked. Our performance that night was nothing to write home about. Then again, he knew we could pull in a crowd. We certainly had that night, anyway. We'd taken a stretch with this one; it was a larger venue than the places we had been playing. Not only that, but rumor had it that if you were going to get picked up by an agency, this was one of the hottest places to be. This could be our ticket.

"That's *awesome*," I told Luke enthusiastically. "We'll have to start drawing up setlists. I feel like we can't keep playing the same thing all the time or it's going to get old. And—"

"Whoa," Luke said, grinning as he held up both his hands. "I'm just as excited and ready to make this work as you are. Can we just enjoy it for a little while before dealing with the logistics, though?"

I chuckled. "Yeah, sure," I said. The truth was that I knew Mark and Carter probably weren't in any shape to change things up. I didn't want to think about that right now, though. I didn't want to let that sour this for me.

What *did* sour my attitude, though, was when I scanned the crowd for my neighbor once more and saw that Carter had cornered her and was leaning in close. I felt a surge of jealousy go through me, and I left Luke where he was, jumping off the stage and making a beeline for the pair. My neighbor looked a little overwhelmed when Carter tried to go in for a kiss, and I hauled him away from her just in time.

I gave him a hard shove. "What the fuck are you doing?" I asked, all the pent-up frustration bursting out of me at once.

Carter looked pissed and shoved me back. "Find your own chick," he snapped. "Or are you just here to be a cock-block again?"

I wanted to punch him, but I knew it wouldn't be fair. It was clear that he was drunk right then, and I doubted that he even knew what he was doing. Fortunately, Luke appeared right then, pulling Carter aside and suggesting that they order some coffee for the next round. The look Carter shot me was murderous, but I doubted he would remember this by the morning.

I grabbed my neighbor's arm and dragged her toward the exit. She giggled. "Nice to meet you too, Caveman," she said. "My name's Leah, what's yours?"

"Jayson," I bit out in a clipped tone.

For some reason, that made her giggle more. I turned toward her as we finally made it out into the night air. As I peered at her, it was obvious she was drunk. Almost as drunk as Carter was. Suddenly, all of my attraction to her evaporated. "You should go home," I told her. "You're going to do something that you regret."

"How do you know what I'd regret?" Leah asked, leaning toward me, her hand resting on my chest, no doubt for balance purposes. She didn't seem too steady on her feet.

"You're drunk," I told her flatly.

Leah laughed. "Isn't that the point of coming to a bar?" she asked, stepping away from me and doing a little twirl that caused her to stumble. But she righted herself and grinned at me.

"It's not safe," I told her, feeling suddenly protective of her. God, I didn't know where she had moved here from, but there was something so innocent about her. It made me even more angry about what might have happened back there. "If I hadn't grabbed Carter off of you, he'd have his mouth glued to yours right now."

Leah shrugged. "He's not that bad-looking," she said. "I could do worse."

I growled, my jealousy flaring up again. I had planned on just sticking her in a taxi, but now I didn't want to leave her alone. Who knew what she might do?

I pulled out my phone and ordered a ride, then texted Luke to break down the equipment without me. I felt bad since I knew it would take him a little while. It wasn't like Carter or Mark would step in to help. But I'd get Luke back at one of the other shows.

"Get in," I said to Leah when the car pulled up to the curb.

"What if I don't want to?" she asked, a teasing challenge in her voice. The look I gave her shut her up, though, and she meekly got into the car. She wasn't quiet for long, though.

"You know, I really liked the show tonight," she said. "The music was good. You're actually a pretty good drummer. But your lead singer talks too much for anyone to really get into it, and then there's the set list. You come out on the highest-energy song, which is good for getting the crowd into it, and then you close on a high-energy song too. But in the middle, things just kind of slow down. It honestly gets kind of boring at points."

I stared at her, mouth agape as she picked us apart. Normally, I would be annoyed. Even more so because I knew that everything she was saying was true. It was part of why I had been trying to get some new material into our shows, because I knew we needed another couple of really banging songs. How was I supposed to get them when Mark and Carter weren't prepared to even play our tried-and-true older stuff?

Somehow, though, I couldn't feel upset with Leah for the way she pointed all of it out. She was just too adorable about it, earnestness in her face like she really wanted to help me out.

I shook my head and didn't respond. She chattered on about something else, the girls that she had been there with, the reason behind the number of shots she had taken, and her current state of drunkenness. I only half-listened, my mind fixed on the band.

I knew we had to break out of this spiral. We couldn't keep going down this road with the way things currently were. If we did, I knew there was no way I was going to achieve my dream of making it big.

There were two options: either Mark and Carter needed to be replaced, or else they needed to shape up and start putting in the effort again. The first didn't really seem like an option, but then again, neither did the second. I felt sick at the thought that my dreams of touring, of crowds who really knew and connected with our music, might die in some dive bar in LA. I didn't want to be just another washed-up bar band.

We finally made it back to our duplex, and I escorted Leah to her door. She looked around in surprise, like she had suddenly realized, just now, that she was no longer at the bar. She started to pout. "Hey, I was having a good time until you came along," she complained. "I wasn't ready to go home yet. I didn't even say goodbye to everyone!"

"Tough," I said, reaching in her pocket to grab her keys and unlock her door. "Go inside, drink some water, and get some sleep."

Leah frowned but headed inside, flicking on the light and grumbling about me, her "overgrown babysitter," as she kicked her shoes off. I was just about to go home, my good deed done, when she muttered, "Thanks to you, I didn't even get to make out with a hot rock star tonight."

Something surged inside of me, and my restraint broke. I knew that it wasn't right to take advantage of her like this, no more than it would have been right to let Carter kiss her when she was drunk. Actually, it was even worse since I was still sober and had my wits about me.

Reason couldn't hold me back now, though. I had wanted her too much all evening to let her go like that. I grabbed her and kissed her, pouring all of my lust, worry, and frustration into the kiss. If she wanted to make out with a rock star, then I was what she got.

She gasped, opening her mouth to me, and I thrust my tongue inside, expecting at any moment for her to push me away. Instead, she melted into my arms, kissing me back just as passionately, moaning as I nipped at her lower lip and tilting her head to the side to give me better access. She wasn't holding anything back, and I kissed her until we were both breathless, and I was hard again.

I could taste the alcohol from the shots she had been doing, and that was what finally sobered me up. I pulled back, shaking my head as her lips chased mine. I tried to find something to say to her, but I wasn't about to apologize. I wasn't sorry for what happened, I just knew that things couldn't go any further.

"Get some sleep," I told her.

Leah scowled, but I turned away from her and went back to my own place, trying not to think about the other course of action I could have taken. It would have been only too easy to let her lead me inside. It would have been only too easy to take her.

But it wouldn't have been right. And at the end of the day, that wasn't the kind of guy I wanted to be. I didn't want to be like Mark or Carter. I wanted to focus on the band and make good music. I didn't need a distraction, especially not one who lived next door to me.

I leaned back against my door, breathing hard. My breathing wasn't the only thing that was hard at the moment. I groaned, pushing my hand down my pants, body jolting with energy as I wrapped my fingers around myself. There was no relief in that sort of release tonight, though.

I stumbled into the living room and sat down at my drums. Surely she was drunk enough that she wouldn't hear me tonight.

Except that if she did, she would be back on my doorstep, and I knew that I wouldn't be able to hold myself back a second time. I got up and went to take a long, cold shower.

6

LEAH

I couldn't help but feel disappointed as Jayson pulled away from me and went back to his own place. "But that's what you get with rock stars," I muttered bitterly as I headed to my room alone. "Flakes, the whole lot of them."

You couldn't count on them. I knew that was true when it came to anything long-term. I just hadn't realized that it also applied to one-night stands. I had thought that they were pretty sure on that. There was so much I didn't know or understand about the lifestyle in LA. I had thought that the longer I lived here, the more I would feel like I was fitting in and understanding it all. Instead, I just felt more out of my element with each passing day.

Face it, you're never going to belong here, I thought sadly as I sat down on the edge of my bed.

I thought back to the kiss with Jayson. For one wonderful moment, I had thought that we might be on the same page. That he might carry me up the stairs and throw me down on the bed and ravish me with his mouth, his hands, his cock.

Instead, he'd pulled back, looking like he regretted kissing me in the first place. And the worst part was that I didn't know what I'd done to make him run out of there like that.

I brushed my fingertips across my lips, narrowing my focus to just the kiss and not what had happened afterward. The kiss had been phenomenal. I had never felt such a frisson of passion inside of me before. His lips guided mine firmly; his tongue delved authoritatively into my mouth. He had held me close, his hard body pressed up against my curves, and I hadn't been able to help the way I had gasped and moaned, pleasure licking through every inch of my body.

I had thought that Carter was going to kiss me earlier in the night, in the bar. I would have welcomed that too; I hadn't been lying to Jayson when I said I could do worse. At the same time, I couldn't deny that Jayson was the one I was attracted to the most.

I wanted him badly.

The kiss had ended too soon, though, and with him babying me again. Did he think I didn't realize I was drunk? I knew I should get some rest; I knew I should drink some water. I knew I'd had one too many shots. At the same time, I was a grown woman. I knew how to take care of myself, and I didn't need him to decide when it was time for me to go home and go to bed.

I shook my head, unable to help feeling unfulfilled and cranky. I yanked off all of my clothes and fell back in bed. I lay there for a moment, thinking of the injustice of it all. It was as though since coming to LA, I was playing along with kids who had learned a different rulebook than me.

But then, I rolled onto my side, curling around a pillow. Was it really that, though? I could lie to myself and say that Jayson had some ulterior plan that I didn't understand, but really I knew that rejection was rejection. Same as back home. It was clear that the rock star wasn't interested in a girl like me. He was way out of my league.

Anyway, it was probably a good thing. Our lifestyles were completely different. I didn't have time for whatever I had wanted with him. I needed to focus on my job, the whole reason I had come here to LA.

Fortunately, I didn't have long to dwell on things before unconsciousness stole over me. My sleep was far from restful, but at least it was sleep.

The next day, I felt like death. I was fortunate to not have any meetings going on early that morning because I was seriously doubting my ability to do anything productive before noon. I shook my head. Back home, I never would have done anything like this. I felt embarrassed as I thought about the fact that everyone else was probably feeling fine and dandy that morning, or at least able to pull it together enough to get in to the office and do their job.

I stumbled blearily into the kitchen to make coffee, feeling as though everything took extra long with the state that I was in. The coffee had just finished brewing when there was a knock on the door. I stared blankly at the clock for a moment without really registering it. Seven o'clock in the morning. Who the hell would be knocking on my door at seven o'clock in the morning?

I finally made up my mind to go find out, half expecting that whoever it was would have left by the time I made it there. When I saw Jayson standing there, I did a double-take. "What?" I asked in confusion.

Jayson grinned and handed me a to-go mug. "Hangover cure," he said, winking at me.

I stared at him for another minute, then decided that I was too hungover to hang on to some semblance of pride by lying that I was fine. I wasn't fine. I was so far from fine that I was willing to try almost anything.

"Drink it," Jayson coaxed me. "It'll help, I promise. I swear by it."

I shook my head and then took a hesitant sip. I grimaced at the flavor. "What the hell is in this?" I asked, barely managing to swallow it down.

Jayson grinned. "You don't want to know," he said. "But I'm not just fucking with you, it really will help."

I seriously doubted that, but there was something in me that was touched by the fact that he had gone out of his way to bring it over to me. He genuinely did seem to care.

"What are you doing here?" I finally asked.

"I wanted to figure out a drumming schedule that's going to work for both of us," he said. "I know that you have to go to work soon probably, and I had some stuff I need to do today too. This will be quick, though."

I frowned at him, wondering at his change in attitude. Maybe last night had made some sort of an impression on him. *Or maybe he's just not the asshole you originally thought he was, and he was only being defensive because you were kind of bitchy when you went over there.*

I stepped back to let him in, leading him toward the kitchen. I took one more sip of the disgusting hangover cure and gagged, putting the cup down on the edge of the counter. "Not gonna happen," I muttered, grabbing a coffee mug and pouring myself some of the dark elixir. "This is my hangover cure."

Not that I'd ever really needed one before. I had gotten

drunk a few times in college. I wasn't that much of a good girl. It hadn't been a ton of fun to actually be drunk, though, and I generally stopped before I hit my limit.

Jayson was grinning when he turned back to me. But his expression quickly turned serious. "I'm used to drumming whenever I feel like it," he said. "I respect that you have a normal job, though. I was thinking that maybe we could reach some kind of compromise. I'm willing to pay for noise-canceling headphones so that you don't have to listen to me."

He said it like it was a done deal. Like it was the obvious solution and like I would be unreasonable if I tried to argue with him.

"Why should I be the one to change my lifestyle because *you're* used to drumming whenever you feel like it?" I snapped, putting my hands on my hips. Whatever good feelings I might have had about him, they were gone now, just like that. What an ass. "*I'm* used to living in peace and quiet."

"Well, maybe you should have thought that before you moved to LA from wherever the hell it is you're from," Jayson said, folding his arms across his chest, now equally annoyed.

For a long moment, we stared one another down, neither of us willing to give an inch. I couldn't help but feel that the tension between the two of us was one of the hottest things I had ever experienced.

7

JAYSON

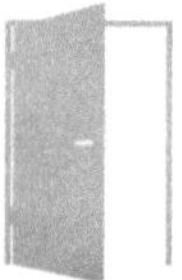

I stared down at Leah. I had to admit, it was definitely a turn-on to hear her stand up for herself like that. She definitely had an attitude about her, but on the other hand, there was something sexy about a woman who could fight back.

She finally shook her head, looking away first. "Look, I respect the fact that drumming is your job," she said. "But I work more hours than most people do. I don't have a nine-to-five; I frequently have more like an eight-to-six. Sometimes more, depending on the week. I need my sleep to keep my brain fresh."

"So what, you think your job is more important than mine?" I gritted out. I didn't mean to sound so harsh, but I was sick of people who wrote me off because musicianship wasn't a "real" job. There was a part of me that knew that people like Mark and Carter were part of the problem. I worked hard, though. I practiced and kept myself in shape and sat down to write lyrics even on days when I would much rather be doing something else. And playing music paid my bills.

Leah sighed and shook her head. "It's not that," she said. "Just, I moved here because of my job. I need to take it seriously or else I don't even know what I'm doing here." She paused. "Anyway, I can't exactly sleep in noise-canceling headphones. They're not comfortable. And I don't want to listen to music or anything like that. I want peace and quiet. Can't you do something to make your drums quieter? Or rent a studio or something?"

I snorted. "Do you have any idea how expensive it would be to rent a music studio in LA?"

"Fair enough," Leah said evenly. "But what about making the drums quieter?"

"I could get drum pads," I finally admitted. "They won't have the same effect, though. I'm not just drumming to try to perfect my skills."

"Then what are you drumming for?" Leah asked wearily.

I shrugged, feeling suddenly embarrassed. Why should I, though? I didn't care what she thought about me. "It's a way for me to work out my energy," I told her. "To decompress and to process what's going on in my life." I expected her to sneer at me and say something about my intellect or something.

Instead, Leah cocked her head to the side, looking thoughtful. "I guess I respect that," she said. "Everyone needs to process. But can't you do something else?"

"Like what?" I asked blankly.

She threw her hands in the air, clearly losing patience with me. Well, damn it, I was losing patience with her as well. She was acting like the problem was all mine. I had lived here for years now without having any sort of problem.

"Therapy?" she suggested. "Join a gym? I don't know."

I scowled at her. I couldn't believe she was being so unreasonable. Here I was, trying to meet her halfway, but she had to compromise too. I shouldn't have to get a studio or find something outside of the house to occupy myself. If I was going to have to change the way I lived in my own house, then she was going to have to as well.

"Clearly we're not going to come up with a solution," Leah said dryly. "Why don't you go? I need to get ready for work."

"That's it?" I snapped. "You're not even willing to find some sort of solution?"

"You want a solution?" she shot back. "How about this: you can drum all day if you want, but at night, you have to be quiet. Just like it says in the lease."

"That's not fair," I said angrily.

Leah grimaced, massaging her temples. "No, what isn't fair is the pounding headache that I have right now and the fact that I have to go to work, like, *now*. I'm not in the mood for this, and I don't see why we need to do it now. You knew I was going to be hungover."

"Not in the mood for it," I said sarcastically. "Well, you were certainly in the mood for *it* last night. From whoever would give it to you."

Leah jerked back as though I had slapped her, and I instantly regretted saying that. We'd all had our nights, and I could only imagine the kind of stress she was under, moving to a new place and starting a new job. She had just been trying to unwind. I knew how that felt.

Besides, I knew that part of why I threw that in her face was that I was still jealous of the fact she had nearly let Carter kiss her first.

"You're a jerk," she said, trying half-heartedly to show me toward the door.

I caught her wrists, only intending to keep her from shoving me. If she wanted me out, I would go under my own speed. But she looked up at me at that moment, her eyes widening as they connected with mine, and I felt that same jolt of electricity inside me.

I didn't know who moved first, but the next thing I knew, I was kissing her hard. I couldn't help myself. I knew it was inappropriate, especially in light of what I had just said. She was too close to me, though, her body pressed up against mine, and I couldn't bring myself to pull away. I was much too turned on to think straight, much too turned on to do the right thing.

And she wasn't complaining, so why the hell was I trying to control myself anyway? I gave in to my lust, letting instinct take control.

8

LEAH

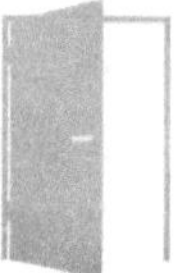

I didn't know how we had gone from fighting to this, but I definitely knew that I wasn't going to stop it. If I had thought the previous night's kiss had been scorching hot, it was nothing compared to this. I couldn't think; I was consumed by desire. Before I realized it, he had me up on the countertop and was standing between my legs, undoing my robe, his hands sliding up my thighs and then up my sides, toying with my bare breasts.

His touches were only featherlight traces of sensation across my skin, but still I felt overcome with the feeling of it all. I arched into him, wanting more, but he continued to tease me, smiling against my lips.

I was so mad at him, so infuriated by the fact that he seemed to think only of himself.

I thought back to the previous night's rejection, trying to summon back all the rational thoughts that had come in the wake of that: thoughts about my career, about how inappropriate this was since he was my neighbor and since I didn't

44

know anything about him. Had it really been rejection, though, or was he really just looking out for me at a time when I was too drunk to do what was best for myself?

Should I stop him from doing this now? I didn't know that I could if I wanted to.

I gasped as his lips slipped away from mine, nibbling at my jawline and then moving lower. He kept his heated gaze upon me as he licked and nipped at my nipple, making the nub stand out from the flesh like a smooth pebble. He rolled that sensitive bit of skin between his fingertips, and this time I wasn't arching because the touch wasn't enough but because it was so damned good.

My legs automatically fell open even wider. I had forgotten all about time, all about the need to get to work. My focus zeroed in on Jayson and the things he could do to my body. The things he *was* doing to my body.

I moaned with need. Jayson answered with a sexy, dangerous grin. He knew just what he could do with a girl. He no doubt knew just how wet I already was, entrance slicked for him to breach.

He wasn't there yet, though. He wasn't through with his teasing.

I knew that like this, he could get me to agree to nearly anything. I wondered if that was all part of his plan: come over here while I was too hungover to really fight him; then when that didn't work, get me so turned on that I could barely breathe, let alone think.

Still, even though I doubted how trustworthy his motives were, I couldn't bring myself to pull away. I wanted this bad. And I needed it even more.

I clung to the edge of the countertop as he found his way between my legs. I lifted my hips as he tugged my panties down away from my slick folds. He nuzzled between my legs, and I bit back a needy little whimper, not wholly successfully. Where before his tongue had explored every inch of my mouth, he now pressed it into my entrance, seeming intent on mapping out every inch of me.

He slid his fingers into my opening as his tongue moved up along my folds, trailing sensually over my clit. I swore and wrapped my legs around his shoulders, urging him on with no thought to anything except the pleasure that he was giving me.

I barely heard the sound of knocking out front, but Jayson yanked back immediately. It took me a second to realize that someone out there was yelling his name.

I dragged my robe hastily closed even though it wasn't as though whoever it was would realize that Jayson was here and come bursting inside. Still, I couldn't help but feel embarrassed. Now that I was back to reality, I realized just how late it was getting. I needed to get to work. Besides, did I really want to go down this path? Jayson was hot as anything, but all my apprehensions from before had come flooding back.

Who did I think I was kidding? He was a rock star. He was way out of my league. Even if he had been the one to start the kiss last night, even if he seemed like he was interested in me, I knew that it was only because there was no one else there in front of him. This was just a matter of convenience, because I happened to be right next door to him.

And surely once he'd had me, he would move on to other ladies. This was just a one-time thing, and I didn't do one-time things.

Whoever had interrupted us, they were still out there, pounding on Jayson's door and shouting his name. The man sounded drunk. I wondered if he was still drunk from the night before or if he had already gotten started on his day. Either way, it was a cold reminder of the world that Jayson lived in. A world that I wanted nothing to do with.

Jayson grimaced and sighed. "Sorry," he said, straightening up. "I'd better go deal with him."

There was a part of me that wanted to beg him to ignore it and go back to what he'd been doing before, but I knew better than to do that. No, it was better that he leave and that we forget all about this.

Still, I couldn't stop myself from going to the window to watch him deal with the drunk guy. I realized with a jolt that it was the guitarist, the one I had almost kissed the night before. Carter. I half expected him to pick up where he had left off the night before, shoving Jayson and yelling about what a cockblock he was.

But of course, if I had been drunk, Carter had been two steps drunker at the very least. He probably didn't remember me or the previous night at all.

I shook my head. If I was this hungover, I could only imagine how the man would feel once he sobered up.

"Come on," I heard Jayson say. "Let's go inside. You need to sleep it off."

Surprisingly enough, Carter followed meekly inside after him. I frowned, still watching as Jayson closed the door behind himself. I remembered how protective he had been the night before. Now, he had shown that same sort of calmness and concern for his friend. Maybe there was more to my new neighbor than met the eye. Maybe I should give him a chance.

Maybe he wasn't just some asshole drummer who would move on to the next girl before my bed was even cold.

There was definitely a part of me that wanted to give

him that chance, to get to know him better and to see where this could go. I had never been more turned on by anyone before. What was I missing out on? The only way to know was to give this a shot.

For a moment, I stood there indecisively. Then, I shook my head. I was already going to be late getting in to work. Even though there was no one checking what time I came in, I had a lot of things that needed to get done. If I wanted to move up in the company, I needed to impress everyone with how dedicated I was to my position.

No more dillydallying thinking of rock stars and sex. I had a career to focus on. If I let that go down the drain, then there was no point in being here at all.

9

JAYSON

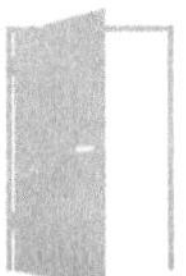

I could have killed Carter for his interruption that morning. All day, I couldn't get out of my mind how hot Leah had been, sitting up on her countertop like that and begging me for more. She had a scent that drove me wild, and I knew instantly that I could never get enough of the taste of her.

I had never felt so invested in pleasing someone before. Maybe it was just that she was so vocal about what she wanted, her whole body showing me just what she needed more of, from the way she moved into my ministrations to the way that she whimpered and gasped when I'd gotten her close.

I had wanted her to come, to watch her fall apart, to feel her body shudder as it was rocked by pleasure. As for me, I had been achingly hard just going down on her, and I'd been so ready to slide into her once I got her off once... or maybe twice.

I'd had to walk out on those ideas, all because Carter

was drunk and couldn't remember the way back to his place. I couldn't resent him for it, though. To be honest, I was too worried about him. I had never seen him like that before, and I felt bad for all my mean thoughts about him lately. Clearly there was something really wrong, and I'd had my head so far up my ass worrying about making it big that I hadn't even noticed.

He was sleeping now on the couch in my living room while I tiptoed around my place. There was a part of me that wanted to go knock on Leah's door, but I knew there was no way she was home right now anyway. She must have gone off to work at some point. And given how seriously she took her job, if she had gotten there late, she would no doubt stay there just as late, making sure that she still put a full day in.

I couldn't help but want to pick up where we had left off, though.

I was surprised by the light knock on my door late that afternoon. For a moment, I couldn't help but just stare at Leah. She was holding a pizza box in her hand, and as I left her standing there, she arched an eyebrow at me, smirking. "Just going to keep me waiting?" she asked, and I had a feeling she wasn't just talking about the fact that she was still standing there on my front stoop.

I wanted nothing more than to yank her into my arms and pick up where we had left off that morning. But Carter was still sleeping on my couch just behind me, and the last thing I needed was for him to wake up, see me with Leah, and remember me shoving him away from her the night before. I could only imagine how that would go down.

So I took a step back, letting Leah inside and letting her see that I wasn't alone. She glanced at Carter and then turned back to me, holding out the pizza. "I figured I owed you dinner since you were kind enough to try to cure my hangover earlier," she explained.

"You didn't have to do that," I said, even though at the same time, I couldn't help but wonder if that was just an excuse to come see me. Maybe she had been thinking about me the same way I had been thinking about her.

Still, there was no way it was going to happen with Carter there on the couch. There was enough tension in the band without adding that to the mix. Until I knew if he remembered me cockblocking him the night before, I couldn't let him know about Leah and me.

"Why don't we go over to your place so we don't wake him up?" I suggested quietly, gesturing at Carter.

Leah grinned at me. "Sounds like a plan," she agreed. "At least until he starts banging on your door again."

I rolled my eyes. "I'm not letting him interrupt us again," I growled. Leah's eyes went dark with lust, but she simply turned and led the way over to her place.

My mind was definitely not on the pizza as we sat eating at her small table. I kept flashing back to the taste of her and flashing ahead to what might come in just a little while.

My mind flashed back to those helpless little noises she had made that morning, the moans and the gasps and the whimpers. She had fallen apart at the way I had touched her, and I wanted to do more.

I was also beginning to realize that she wasn't my usual type at all. She wasn't the free-spirit, free-love kind of groupie girl that came to our shows. She was a little uptight, a little high-strung. Getting her to relax, watching her fall apart, was intoxicating.

It wasn't just my physical attraction to her, either, honestly. It was also the fact that she was smart. And as she chattered away during dinner, apparently nervous, I had to admit she was funny as well.

There were so many things about her that drove me wild, and I wasn't going to pass up the chance to get to know her better. I finished a slice of pizza and pushed my plate away slightly, looking over at her. The food had been satisfying, but not as satisfying as it had been to lay my hands on her earlier in the day.

Leah's breath hitched as I stared at her, an undisguised hunger in my eyes. She slowly set down her slice of pizza, staring straight back at me. Before I could make a move, though, she stood up, abruptly grabbing both of our plates and carrying them to the sink. She seemed uncertain, like she wanted to give in but wasn't sure that she should. She was fighting it, her uptight nature warring with basic human need.

If she needed persuasion, I could help her out.

I went up behind her, standing close, waiting for her to take a step away. But she didn't. If anything, she leaned closer to me. I slowly brushed her hair off her neck and kissed the soft skin there. She melted back against me with a shuddery exhale.

"I appreciate the pizza, but another taste of you would be much more enjoyable," I murmured against her skin. Maybe it was cheesy, but we were both so caught up in our desires that neither of us seemed to care. I slipped a hand up under her shirt, playing my fingers across her smooth skin.

Suddenly, she pulled away from me, turning around and shaking her head. "This is a bad idea," she warned me.

"Why?" I asked, a challenge in my voice. Oh, I knew all the logical reasons against it. I might not be Carter, but all the same reasons I hadn't wanted her getting involved with him? The same held true for me. I might not mean to break her heart, but I was afraid that I might if I let this continue.

I wasn't going to be here in LA forever, not if I had my way. I was going to make it with the band, and then there were going to be long months of touring. I wouldn't want her just sitting around waiting for me to return. That wouldn't be fair.

She couldn't fit into my life. I wasn't ready to let her go just yet, either, though.

"It's probably not a good idea to get involved with a neighbor," Leah said, shrugging. She looked uncertain.

I rolled my eyes at that lame excuse. "Why not?" I asked. "Anytime you want to borrow a cup of sugar, all you have to do is ask."

Leah stared at me for a moment and then laughed, shaking her head. I could see in her eyes she still had reservations. I knew I had doubts of my own. Neither of us could deny the tension between us, though.

I leaned in toward her, giving her plenty of time to protest again, to turn away. Instead, she met me in the middle, kissing me again. I felt a thrill go through me.

I leaned into the kiss, pulling her even closer against me, already imagining her naked skin pressed to mine. I poured all my passion, every ounce of emotion, into the kiss. As Leah responded with an eagerness of her own, I knew it was going to be a very good time.

LEAH

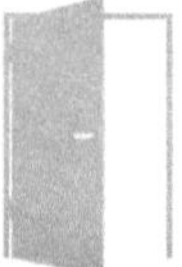

I hadn't been sure if the pizza thing was a good idea. I had spent the whole day trying to focus on my work, but in the back of my mind, I couldn't seem to quit thinking about the best way to conspire to see Jayson again.

There were so many different options. Should I show up at another of his band's shows? But I wasn't a groupie, and I didn't want him to think I was. Nor did I really want to see Carter again and maybe accidentally give him the impression that I was there for him. Besides, I didn't even know the band's name. I hadn't caught it the night before, and I wasn't about to ask Piper or anyone else at work.

That wasn't really any sort of option, unfortunately. So what could I do?

The only other things I knew about Jayson were where he lived and the fact that he was a dude. That didn't give me many options, but dudes were always down for food, weren't they? Besides, it would seem like the perfect response to his attempts to cure my hangover. If he wasn't interested, if nothing else happened, if this morning had been a mistake, then we could forget all about it and move on with our lives.

I didn't think that morning had been a mistake, though. Neither, it appeared, had Jayson.

I knew the minute he followed me back to my place that we were going to pick up where things had left off that morning. We weren't just there so that we could keep from waking up Jayson's bandmate; we were there so that he wouldn't find out that I lived next door, so that he wouldn't find out about Jayson and me.

There was something sexy about sneaking around like that. As though we were doing something truly naughty, something just a little bit dangerous.

I had never been the kind of girl to go for the bad boys, and I had sworn that there was no way that I was going to get with a rock star. But I suppose if you were going to have a fling like that, then LA was definitely the place for it. And Jayson was clearly the one to have a fling like that with.

His experience was immediately apparent. But it didn't make me feel uncomfortable or self-conscious even though I knew that my fumblings back home had nothing on him. The kiss was full of raw heat, passion, and desire and not a single ounce of logic or uncertainty. I leaned into it, gasping as he felt me up through my shirt, his fingers strong and sure.

He grinned against my mouth, like he was amused at how turned on he could get me.

We never made it to my bedroom. Instead, the next thing I knew, I was sprawled out on the couch, Jayson stripping off my clothing and kissing his way along each new inch of my flesh that he uncovered along the way. It was overwhelming, the way he stimulated me. His hands, his lips, his tongue were everywhere all at once. His hot breath made me shiver as it breezed across my naked skin.

I ached to be filled by him, ached to have him pin me down and fuck me, bring me to the brink and carry me over. I had never felt this desperate with desire before. Was it just that no one had focused so intently on me before, or was there something more to it than that?

I trembled as delicious pleasure spilled through me. I had been so close already that morning with his mouth on me, and as much as I had wanted to, I hadn't given in to touching myself, in spite of how much time I had spent thinking about him. I knew that anything else would be unsatisfactory, would only leave me unsated and unfulfilled.

Now, though, I was wondering if maybe it would have been better to give myself that release, even if it wasn't a true release at all. Maybe it would have made me a little less desperate, held me back from the brink for a little bit longer. As it was, I could barely breathe by the time he pressed his cock into me, and it was only a matter of time before we were both throbbing with intense energy.

He thrust his hips and I lifted to meet his movements.

"Jesus, you feel so good Leah," Jayson breathed against my ear.

I locked my legs around his waist and pulled in deeper, my pussy spasming around him as I came apart.

"Yeah, that's it. Just like that," he growled as he continued to fuck me through my orgasm.

I pulled his mouth back to mine and kissed him deeply, his tongue sweeping over mine.

"Harder, please," I begged him as I came up for air.

Jayson lifted himself up on his forearms and looked down at me as he increased the depth and speed of his thrusts. He grabbed one of my legs and rested my ankle on his shoulder, creating a new angle where he could reach my deepest parts.

"Oh God, yes!" I cried as he plunged to dizzying depths.

Suddenly, a new wave of pleasure crested, and I came nearly without warning, my pussy clamping down on him, milking until he couldn't hold back any longer.

Another deep thrust had Jayson roaring on top of me as his cock spasmed and emptied deep inside of me.

He collapsed against me and we lay there for a few minutes, neither of us saying anything.

As my breathing returned to normal and my thoughts stopped swirling, I was overcome by near panic. What had I just done?

I knew that Jayson was not close to my type. That he lived a completely different life than I did and that there was no way we could ever work out. Was getting laid worth the awkwardness and potential heartbreak that would follow if I continued to pursue this?

My anxieties got the better of me, and I climbed off the couch. The earlier feeling I had been dreading, the lack of fulfillment in spite of the orgasm, came creeping up on me. "I have a thing this evening," I told him vaguely.

It was a lie. I didn't have any plans, and I wanted nothing more than to melt back into his arms and let him shelter me from the world. I knew that I couldn't, though. That wasn't an option.

I was surprised to see Jayson's face harden. He stood up, his whole body tense. I ducked my head, feeling ashamed, not entirely sure what was happening but knowing that I didn't like the feeling. There was a part of me that wanted call after him as he straightened his clothes without a word and headed for the door.

The words stuck in my throat, though. I trailed silently after him. Inside my head, I was begging him to say something, anything.

At the last moment, he turned toward me. For the briefest second, there was a flash of regret on his face, a certain tenderness. I held my breath, wishing he would reach out and caress my cheek, brush my hair back, maybe kiss me again. Just because this couldn't happen again, it didn't mean that it had to end this way, with ice between us.

These feelings that I had for him were exactly the reason it could never happen again. God, how was I already so caught up in his web? I barely knew the guy. This was only a one-time thing; I had known that going into it. No point making it into something it wasn't.

Then, Jayson shook his head slightly, one single and sharp movement. I couldn't tell if it was a response to something on my face or if he was trying to negate something inside of his head. "Thanks for the pizza," he said. With that, he turned to leave.

I slumped there in the front hall, wondering if I had just screwed everything up. The truth was I had nowhere to be that night. Except that now, since he lived next door, I felt like I had to go out, just to preserve the lie. I immediately felt tired. But what else could I do?

I sighed but texted Piper, hoping she might be free. I didn't know what else to do. I had no one to meet, since I barely knew anyone in town yet. The other girls had been nice the night before, but I certainly didn't know any of them well enough to text them.

I just hoped they weren't out at another club. I didn't

know if I could take another night of drinking. I already still felt off after the night before.

My phone buzzed almost immediately with a reply from Piper.

No plans, but this is the perfect time to show you some of LA since you're new here!

I texted her back: *What did you have in mind?*

I couldn't help but think back to the way it had felt to be tangled up in Jayson's arms on the couch. That was where I would much rather be right now, but I tried to shake that thought out of my head. That wasn't an option.

I frowned down at my phone as it buzzed with another text: *It's a surprise. Dress casual, pick you up at your place. Text me the address.*

I wrinkled my nose. The last thing I wanted was a surprise. On the other hand, I could use the distraction. Maybe it would keep me from thinking about Jayson's strong, tattooed arms and the way he had fit so perfectly inside of me.

I headed to the bathroom to shower, then got dressed semi-casually in a sexy, low-cut top and dark jeans, figuring I was covering all my bases that way if we were going to a club or something.

I couldn't help but wonder what Jayson would think of my outfit. No doubt it was tame and unremarkable next to the outfits of the girls was used to hanging out with. I had seen how the girls were dressed the night before at their show. All those groupies had been wearing something that was only a step away from lingerie.

Was I jealous? Did I regret sleeping with him?

For a moment, I paused there in the shower, the soap still clutched in my hand. Did I regret sleeping with him?

To be honest, I couldn't. The sex had been amazing. But whatever had happened between Jayson and me was over.

I shouldn't be upset about that, anyway. He wasn't the kind of man I saw myself with long-term, no matter how good the sex had been, and I was pretty sure the feeling was mutual. Still, now that I'd gotten my first LA fling, and indeed my first real fling *ever* out of the way, maybe I'd be able to focus on the things that really mattered.

Like work and building my connections there. As Piper pulled up out front, I fixed a smile on my face. Maybe we couldn't talk about work outside of work, but that didn't mean I couldn't make friends. I had a feeling Piper was one of those people who knew a little bit of everything that there was to know about our coworkers, and that could make her invaluable as I moved up in the company.

That was what I was here for, after all—not rock stars. I was here for my work, and that was the way things would stay.

1 1

—

JAYSON

I tried not to be pissed off as I went back to my place. I wasn't used to having the girl kick me out. I especially wasn't used to having a girl kick me out so she could get together with another guy. Leah hadn't told me that that was what she was up to that night, but then again, she hadn't not told me, either. Besides, it was pretty easy to connect the dots. Why else would she be so vague about her plans?

Not only that, but I couldn't pretend like I was surprised. Sure, she had been maddeningly close to Carter the night before, and she had said that thing about wanting to be with a rock star. At the end of the day, though, we came from two different worlds. I wasn't her type. She was too uptight and prissy for me.

I had revised my opinion of her after our initial meeting. Now, I wondered if I had been too hasty on that.

I tried to imagine the type of dude she would normally go for. Or the type of *dud* she would normally go for, rather.

Still, some smart, put-together, career-minded man probably suited her a lot better than I ever could. It was no wonder she rushed me out of there immediately after having sex with her. She probably had a date with her Prince Charming that evening, and she needed to wash my scent off of her.

There was a part of me that wondered if the only reason I was so disgruntled about the whole thing was that I could tell that she didn't sleep with guys too often and I was pissed to know that she apparently didn't think too highly of her time with me. Or was it just that I couldn't get out of my head how good it had been for myself, and I assumed it must have been just as good for her, at least until she kicked me out of there. I knew she'd come at least twice. I had felt it.

I shook my head. Dwelling on this kind of shit wasn't like me. True, I didn't go home with that many ladies. I didn't have many one-night stands. Still, I knew what a one-night stand was, and I knew better than to go mooning after them after things were clearly done.

There was a part of me that couldn't help but wonder if I had expected something different from this one. I didn't want to examine that too closely, though.

Once back in my side of the duplex, I shook Carter awake, nothing better to do. Besides, we should get at least a little practice today. Or if practice with the full band was going to be impossible, then I needed to practice my drums alone.

Now, while I had the chance—while Leah was headed out. *With some guy.*

Carter blinked up at me, bleary-eyed. "You should take a shower," I grunted, handing him a mug of coffee because I wasn't a heartless bastard.

Carter took a couple sips of coffee as he woke up, looking around himself in surprise. "What am I doing here?" he asked blankly.

I shrugged. "You showed up this morning," I explained. "I think you wanted to keep the party going, but I convinced you to crash instead."

There was a lot more than that I wanted to say. This wasn't the first time Carter had shown up at my place as he tried to outrun his demons. It wasn't the first time he had blacked out, or the first time he had passed out on my couch. I had kind of thought it would get old after a while, but that didn't seem to be the case.

Carter nodded, running a hand through his hair. "Honestly, I don't remember much after last night's show," he admitted. I hoped that meant he didn't remember Leah and the way he had almost kissed her.

Not that it mattered either way. I didn't have any claim on her. Not that I wanted someone like Carter fucking around with her, though.

"Maybe it's time you considered laying off the booze," I couldn't help but say.

Carter stared at me for a long moment. From the flat set to his mouth, I could tell there were a dozen things he wanted to say in response to that. He held them all back, though. I didn't know if I was thankful for that. There was a part of me that couldn't help but wonder—if he and I really went at it, shouted at each other, finally aired all of our grievances, would it help us finally start to put ourselves back together again? Would it fix some of the tension within the band?

But he was silent, and I had already said too much. If I just kept pushing him, I would destroy everything.

He drained his coffee mug and set it down on the coffee

table, scrubbing his hands over his face. "Can I grab a shower?" he asked.

"Sure," I said. He headed into the bathroom, and I sat down at my drum set.

I grabbed my sticks and played a slow roll on the cymbal. But I left it at that, too distracted to actually put something together.

It was all Leah's fault that I couldn't concentrate. If she hadn't been at the show the night before, if she weren't so cute... If she hadn't been so damned sexy, with the way she reacted to every touch of my fingers and mouth against her skin. It was just a fling with my next-door neighbor, but I couldn't get her out of my head.

I knew I needed to focus on my music. It was one of the things that had been driving me nuts about the way Carter and Mark were acting lately. The last thing I needed was to forget all about my goals in pursuit of a pretty woman. Even if that pretty woman lived next door to me and was impossible to ignore.

There was a part of me that wished she hadn't shown up there with pizza that evening, regardless of what it had led to. There was a bigger part of me that just couldn't get over what had happened. I had never expected her to blow my mind. I wondered how I could possibly keep my hands off her now.

Even if she clearly would rather be with someone else.

Carter came out of my bedroom before my blood could boil over with jealousy. He was pulling one of my T-shirts over his head. I knew I would never get it back.

That was the thing—I knew exactly how these sorts of situations with Carter always ended. And yet somehow, we still kept ending up back here.

Was that the only thing that drew me to Leah? The fact

that she was unpredictable, the fact that she was the only new and different thing in my life at the moment? I wanted to think that wasn't all it was, but at the end of the day, I wasn't so sure.

Carter and I headed for the taco truck up the street, as we always did after one of his benders. Suddenly, I was just so sick of the predictable.

"You know," I said, trying to sound casual, "I don't know how much you remember from last night, but we were really good. Crowd was really into it."

Carter made a noncommittal noise. I wondered how much of what I was saying were things he was choosing not to hear. I wondered why it was that now, when we were so close, was the time that he and Mark both seemed dead set on sabotaging us.

I felt myself starting to get annoyed. "If we keep booking shows at the rate we've been going, it's only a matter of time before we make it big," I said. "Or at least bigger. It's going to take an effort from all the members, though." Carter still didn't seem to be paying attention, focusing more on his tacos than on me. "We could make better money," I added, wondering if that was the trick.

Still no response. Finally, I shook my head, deciding that the personal appeal I'd been holding back had a place after all. I leaned forward.

"Even if the band goes down in flames, I'm your friend," I said quietly. "You know that if you don't stop, you're risking permanent damage."

We all saw where things were headed, I was sure. Somehow, no one else seemed to care.

I knew it wasn't that, though. It wasn't that no one cared. It was just that no one else was willing to put themselves in the crosshairs to call him out. Luke especially wasn't, and Mark was nearly as far down as Carter, albeit in different ways.

"Carter, you need help," I said, unable to bite back the words even though I knew they wouldn't be appreciated. "Look, I'll go to a meeting with you if that's what it takes. You can't keep..." I trailed off.

Carter scowled at me. "Don't pretend like you don't have any vices," he snapped. He stood up. "If you want to practice at all today, we should get going," he said in a clipped tone. "If you want to catch Mark before he goes out, anyway."

I stared at him for a moment, not wanting to let the conversation die. I wondered if there was any way to get him to listen. Admit to my own faults and get him to admit to his. Instead, though, I got to my feet and silently followed him. I didn't know how to get through to him, and I was afraid that the more I needled him, the further away I would push him.

LEAH

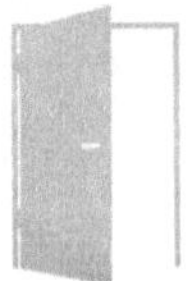

I looked around in surprise, taking in the sights and sounds. "Where is this?" I asked Piper, in awe of the colored lights and foreign chatter around us. For a moment, it was as though I wasn't even in California anymore. For someone like me, from a small town in the middle of nowhere, someone who had never traveled before, it was unreal.

Piper laughed at my expression. "I had a feeling you might think this was cool," she said. "Best night market in LA."

I shook my head, unable to help but marvel at everything. It definitely beat noisy clubs and terrible dive bars.

"Come on," Piper said, grabbing my arm and tugging me along. "I'm hungry. And I'm looking for one of those colorful silk scarves to wear to work on Monday."

I laughed and followed her into the press of people, trying my best not to feel too overwhelmed by all of it.

"So how do you like the new job?" Piper asked a little

while later as we munched on snacks from one of the booths.

I raised an eyebrow at her. "I thought we couldn't talk about work outside of work," I said.

Piper shrugged and laughed. "Up to you," she said. "That's really just Linsey's rule, though. Mainly because she doesn't like her job and doesn't want to think about it anymore than she has to, basically."

I snorted. "I guess that's fair," I said. "I don't know, it's definitely all been an adjustment, but I think it's a good thing. I like the work, and I'm starting to get used to living in LA."

I wasn't, not really, but she didn't need to know that. She didn't need to know that I had slept with my next-door neighbor just to scratch an itch. She didn't need to know that that was the whole reason I had called her tonight, because I needed some sort of excuse to get out of the house after ditching him. For her, a one-night stand was probably no big deal. Just one of those things that you did.

"You're good at the work too. Way better than the last person who had your position," Piper said, rolling her eyes. "Man, I think everyone was relieved when Brandon quit. Not only was he miserable when it came to doing his own work, but he somehow managed to make more work for everyone else as well. Real piece of work."

I giggled. "Well, I'm glad that I'm better than him, at least," I said. "How long have you been with the company anyway?" I asked her.

"It'll be five years this winter," Piper said. She wrinkled her nose. "I never really pictured myself with a career or anything, but they hired me when I was fresh out of college based off an internship I had with them, and I don't know. I like the people, and there's nothing I would rather be doing, even if I don't love every minute of the job itself."

"Hmm, that's fair," I said, frowning as I tried to imagine what that must feel like. But I had always kind of known what I wanted to do with my life. I couldn't imagine just having lukewarm feelings toward my job.

"Anyway, I think if I can really impress everyone at the retreat next month, I might get tapped for a promotion," Piper added. She laughed self-consciously, running her fingers through her hair. "I probably shouldn't tell you about that because I don't know who else is trying to get the position."

"I won't tell anyone," I told her. Because in the first place, who would I tell? Secondly, I didn't have a ton of friends in LA, and the fact that she trusted me enough to tell me about her goals for the future was kind of flattering. I wasn't about to screw that up.

Especially not because if things went well for her, who knew, maybe she could help me move up in the company as well.

"What's this retreat really about?" I asked her curiously. I had heard some rumors of it, but no one really seemed to want to give too many details to me.

Piper shrugged. "The main thing is that it's a chance to get some face time with the big boss," she said. "It's one of the only times all year that we get that chance. So make sure you don't waste it."

I nodded, trying not to feel too intimidated by her words. I wanted to climb the ladder, to work my way up the ladder. That meant I needed to not screw things up with the bosses before I had really made any sort of good impact on the company.

Fortunately, there was another thing to distract me: I

saw a man ahead of us, caught a flash of his tattoos. I knew instantly that it wasn't Jayson, but I couldn't help but feel a tug of lust in my core, a fleeting wish to be back in his arms. I thought back to what had happened earlier, and I wished suddenly that he could be the one here with me at the night market, as much as I liked Piper.

Piper glanced over her shoulder, frowning in puzzlement. "Who'd you see?" she asked.

I shook my head. "No one," I said. "Just thought I saw someone I knew."

Piper raised an eyebrow at me. "Someone from work?"

"No," I said slowly, reluctant to tell her who it really was. I knew that if I admitted I was imagining Jayson there in the market, she would know that something was up.

She wasn't going to let me off so easily, though. "Come on, you can't know that many people in LA that I don't know. And you look like you've seen a ghost. What's up?"

I sighed. "You know that band we went to see?" I realized absently that I still didn't even know their name, but I pressed on before I could dwell on that and all the other things I didn't know about Jayson. "The drummer lives next door to me."

"Well, that's convenient," Piper said, smirking at me. "So are you going to hook up with him? Should we go to another one of his shows or something?"

I coughed lightly. I supposed I shouldn't have been so surprised that she would immediately suggest hooking up with him. This was LA after all. Things were just so different from how they were back home.

"I actually already kind of... hooked up with him," I admitted.

Piper grinned. "Nice!" she said. "He's fucking hot, good for you."

I couldn't help but blush. Somehow, the words kept spilling out of me. Maybe it was just the fact that Piper was really my only friend here, that I had no one to confide in other than her. But I had a feeling it was also that I was looking for guidance from someone.

"I'm kind of conflicted about it," I told her. "I've never just had sex with someone before; I've always been in a relationship first."

Piper frowned. "Do you want to be in a relationship with him?" she asked.

I snorted. "Doesn't matter if I do," I said. "Have you seen him? He's a rock star. I'm sure he sleeps around with a lot of girls."

Piper shook her head. "And none of them have anything on you," she said firmly. "If you want him, you could have him."

"I don't know if I do," I sighed.

"Well, was the sex any good? Did you enjoy it at least?"

I groaned. "Probably too much," I said. Thinking back to it made me shiver, even now. But that wasn't the point, was it?

"I don't think there's any such thing as 'too much,'" Piper said, her eyes twinkling. "So come on, if the sex was good, what's stopping you? Seriously, if you're just worried about the other girls, you're crazy."

"It's not just that," I sighed. "He's just not exactly the man that I thought I'd end up with. I always kind of figured I'd find some guy in finance, or maybe a college professor. Someone who shared my interests." I paused and then grinned crookedly. "Someone who likes quiet nights at home, that sort of thing."

Piper laughed. "I mean, sure," she said. "We're all looking for something more like that eventually, right? You don't have to marry the drummer, though. Just have some fun with him. You're young, and you just moved here. You don't have to settle down just yet."

"I know." I shook my head. "I'm just not sure that I'm ready for no-strings-attached kind of fun. I'm just not cut that way." I was quiet for a moment, looking around. "LA is so, so different from back home, you have no idea."

"Do you miss it?" Piper asked, cocking her head to the side.

"I guess part of me does," I said quietly. "Not all of me, but definitely part of me."

"Fair enough," Piper said. "But I guess, why not just see where things take you? If you decide you're not interested in him anymore, then you can just kick him to the curb, right?"

I shook my head, knowing that there was no way it would be that easy. The further I went down this road, the more difficult it was all sure to become. I already couldn't stop thinking about the guy. The last thing I needed was to start to get attached to him.

"How would I even get him to pick me over the other girls?" I asked. It was one thing for Piper to say I was better than the groupies. She knew me. But Jayson didn't know me, and I wasn't sure that he cared to. I mean, hell, I didn't know anything about him either. It was just sex, and if it was just sex, he wouldn't care if I had a brain and a personality. Right?

"Well, to start with, I think you and I are going to need to go lingerie shopping," Piper said, smiling wickedly. "Something tells me you don't have anything special to wear for the dude, do you?"

I felt another blush stain my cheeks. "Uh, no," I said,

feeling embarrassed. I had never really seen the point of lingerie anyway. Wasn't it just going to come off?

But as I thought about wearing a skimpy lace number for Jayson, I had to admit that there was something about the fantasy that made me feel hot. I could imagine the way he would look at me, the way he would caress me as he marveled at the play of lace across my skin.

"Who could think about groupies if he saw you wearing thigh-high stockings with garters and a tight little corset?" Piper said, still grinning at me.

"I don't know," I said slowly.

"Come on, you have an amazing body," Piper said. "You should show off those curves sometimes."

I felt my blush deepen. I had never had the kind of girly friendship before where we talked about things like that. I had never had the type of friendship where I thought about going lingerie shopping with someone.

"Dress for the position you want, right?" Piper said, winking at me. "That's the whole reason I'm looking for a scarf tonight: I want something sophisticated but also kind of fun, something that made me stand out to everyone."

I shook my head. "And what, wearing lingerie under my clothes to work is going to help me land the position I want?" I asked doubtfully.

Piper laughed. "Look, not all the positions you might want in life are going to be related to your work," she said. "Maybe the position you want is... on top of a sexy drummer."

I burst out laughing, unable to help it. "Sure, maybe," I said.

"So you'll go lingerie shopping with me?" Piper pressed.

I shook my head ruefully. "Sure, maybe," I said. To be honest, I wasn't sure that that was anything I really wanted to do, but I couldn't stop thinking of what it would be like to wear something sexy for Jayson, knowing that I bought it for his eyes only.

Would he realize I had bought it just to wear for him? Did I want him to realize that?

The thought sent a bolt of heat through me. I tried not to dwell on it too much and instead focused on enjoying my night with Piper. I wondered if I would see him when I got home, if he would still be awake or drumming or...

Again, I was trying not to think about any of it. It was difficult, though. Was I developing feelings for him—was it already too late?

13

JAYSON

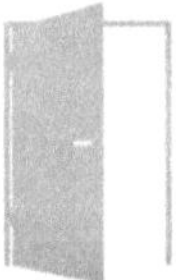

It had been a couple of weeks since the day I'd hooked up with Leah, and I was starting to wonder if she was avoiding me. I mean, Mr. Lake and I hadn't seen one another all the time back when he still lived next door, but we had still crossed paths every so often on the way to the mailbox or leaving the house for the day.

I had barely even seen Leah, though. Once, I had caught a glimpse of her going into her place as I came back from a band practice, but either she hadn't heard me honk the horn or... Well, she hadn't turned around, anyway.

There was a part of me that wanted to go over there and knock on her door. Maybe bring her pizza this time and see if it led to the same results. My eyes kept scanning the crowds at our concerts, looking for her. Our groupies' flirtations held even less appeal to me now.

It wasn't just about the sex, though, although that had been mind-blowing. Things were getting even more intolerable with Mark and Carter, and it was getting to the point where I just needed to talk to someone about all of it. Anyone.

Except for Luke. He had always been the one I talked to about things like that, but he had started withdrawing more and more lately, stewing in his frustrations on his own. I knew that we had to come up with some sort of solution soon or else the whole band was going to implode, but I had no idea what to do. I needed someone who could be objective.

For some reason, Leah stood out as the person I would like to talk to about it. Maybe it was just the fact that I could tell she would have a different perspective than anyone else I knew, or maybe it was the fact since we'd slept together, I couldn't help but feel a certain closeness to her, even though that was a dangerous thought.

Maybe it was the fact that she was so career-driven, herself, and I knew that she would help me see what I wanted more clearly.

In any case, she didn't seem to want to have anything to do with me, and I wasn't sure how to push her for something more. I could tell she had felt awkward after we'd slept together. Sure, she'd had something to do that night, but I could tell it had been more than that.

I wished I could talk to her about it. I would have felt awkward about pounding on her door and demanding some sort of explanation, though. Besides, Carter was over at my place more often than not lately, and I would have felt like a heel turning my back on him so I could focus on what was going on with Leah. After all, we had just had a one-night stand. It wasn't like she and I were in a long-term relationship.

Carter's drinking was really starting to concern me, but not just because it affected the band. He was my friend, more than just a bandmate. I was worried about him.

At first, I had figured that I would go out with him, keep an eye on him and see if I could get him to stop drinking before he got too wasted. That hadn't worked, though. Carter had an explosive temper once he started drinking, and he resented me stopping him from either partying or hooking up with girls.

So afterward, it was mostly trying to steer him toward some of our less-wasted groupies and then convince him to head home at a reasonable hour. Sometimes it worked, sometimes it didn't. And most times, it ended with him showing up on my doorstep hungover (or still drunk) and passing out on my couch.

There was part of me that wanted to just shake him and tell him to shape up. To remind him that our futures were at stake here. Or maybe to even go so far as to toss him in my trunk and drop his ass off at rehab.

I didn't know how to have that conversation, though. Carter was spiraling out of control, but he seemed to be refusing all help at the same time.

That night, we were due to go on in about forty-five minutes. I was setting up my kit on the stage while watching Carter out of the corner of my eye. I grimaced as I watched him laugh and sling an arm around a woman, then take a shot of tequila. He had barely set the glass back on the bar before the bartender was pouring him another one.

Just then, Mark rolled up, a girl on his arm. "Hey, Jayson, you going to go do something to handle Carter before he's too drunk to play?" he asked. I couldn't tell if he was taunting me or actually asking me to go handle Carter.

My hands clenched into fists, and I was just about to retort that maybe Mark should do something himself when he turned his back on me and headed toward the bar with the girl trailing behind.

Probably just as well. All Mark was likely to do would be to exacerbate the situation. Hell, he'd probably start buying Carter more shots. That was the last thing we needed at the moment.

"Need any help with anything? Or anyone?" I looked over, half hoping to see Leah standing there, even though I realized belatedly that it wasn't her voice who had spoken to me.

Instead, it was Trixie standing there. Because of course it was. She was there at almost all of our shows, and even though she was clearly trying to sleep her way through everyone in the band, she seemed pretty intelligent as well. If anyone was going to realize how things really were going for the band, it was her. She knew us at least as well as anyone did.

Somehow, that pissed me off even more, though. I didn't want our band to be known for infighting. I didn't want our struggles to be obvious to outsiders. Why did Mark and Carter not seem to care at all about our image? Why didn't they seem to care about the band?

I just shook my head at her. "Don't worry about it," I told her.

"Yeah, okay," she said, grinning at me. "I'm sure you can handle it, can't you? You're always so good with the two of them."

I bristled slightly. The last thing I needed right now was her flirting with me.

I didn't want to examine why that thought bothered me

so much. But as my eyes scanned the gathering crowd, I knew I wasn't searching for my bandmates' faces.

"Just enjoy the show," I told her brusquely, finishing up on the stage. I headed toward the bar. Mark wasn't even talking to Carter, and I wasn't sure if that was a blessing or a curse as Carter was getting drunker by the minute. Mark, on the other hand, was flirting with the blonde bartender.

I huffed angrily. It was nearly time for soundcheck, and here they were. We were never going to get anywhere like this. But then again, with the way things had been going lately, they probably wouldn't care if our vocals were mute, our guitars out of tune, or anything else we were meant to check prior to the start of the show.

Hell, if I hadn't even gotten Carter's guitar out of its case prior to the show, I doubted that he would have noticed. What the fuck was going on with us?

I grabbed Mark first, my hand landing heavily on his shoulder. "Get Carter, find Luke, and get ready for soundcheck," I said in a clipped tone.

Mark looked for a moment like he wanted to protest, but then he pasted a cocky grin on his face and turned to the bartender. "Guess it's showtime," he said, winking at her as he slipped off his stool and went over to where Carter was listing to one side.

I leaned over toward the bartender. "Cut off the guitarist, okay? He's had enough." It shouldn't have been up to me to ask her to do that, but then again, he had already passed the point of drunkenness, and for whatever reason, she was still serving him.

That was half of the trouble: Carter still had charisma even when drunk. He always seemed to convince them that serving him was in their best interest. I didn't know what he promised them, but he rarely got cut off, and it was starting to drive me crazy.

Sure enough, she raised an eyebrow at me, looking skeptical. "He's one of my best customers," she said.

I scowled at her. "You want me to get a cop in here to breathalyze him?" I snapped. "You realize that it's against the law for you to keep serving him if he's already drunk?"

She pursed her lips tightly. "Fine," she said. "I'll stop serving him. But you can be the one to tell him that because the last thing I need is for him to try to start a fight with me."

I nodded curtly at her, then turned to head back to the stage. Fortunately, the band was assembled, and we were all ready to start our soundcheck.

Things went fine. Not great, but not terribly, either. Muscle memory could take you pretty far, I guess, and we had definitely practiced enough over the years to nail our hits at the very least. We still couldn't add any new material, though, and it was starting to bother me more and more.

We finished up the show, and Luke and I started to break things down. Carter and Mark, of course, headed immediately to the bar. I wondered how long it would be before Carter found out that he wasn't being served anymore and cause a ruckus.

I hated that I had to think that way. I didn't want to be his keeper.

And there was a part of me that knew even if the bartender refused to give Carter a drink, he was going to find a way to get one anyway. From the way the groupies were flocked around them, it was only a matter of time.

"I've been talking to an agent," Luke said suddenly.

I dropped a cymbal with a loud crash, staring at him with wide eyes. Normally, my equipment was more important to me than anything else, and I wouldn't have left anything sitting there on the floor. But what he had just said was way too important.

"What?" I asked dumbly.

"You heard me," Luke retorted. "He gave me a card after our last show up at Bay Heights. He's interested."

I stared at him for a moment and then shook my head. "We're already getting okay gigs," I said. "We should probably focus on that for now, shouldn't we?"

Luke groaned. "If we focus on that, you know we're never going to change. We're never going to get anywhere else," he said. I hated to admit that he was right.

"Well, what did he say?" I finally sighed. This was it, then. This was how things came to a head. We needed to figure out some way to keep moving forward, even if it meant that we had to ditch the other two, reform the band in some other way.

I didn't like to think about that.

"We've got a shot," Luke said, his words dripping with import. "We need a better-quality album to shop around, though." He was quiet for a moment. "I know that you're looking for us to put some more new material into our routine, but to be honest, I think we have enough material. We just need to put it together into a better demo."

I snorted. "What's going to make a better demo is if we don't record it in your basement next time," I pointed out.

"Sure," Luke agreed. A fleeting grin flashed across his face. "What if I said that I could get us into a studio?"

I blinked in surprise. "How?"

Luke shrugged. "Someone owes me a favor," he said.

For a minute, I let myself consider the possibility of it. If only someone had owed him a favor months ago before everything started to go to shit. Now, though, things were different. If we wanted to make the most of our one shot in the studio, we were going to need to get our shit together. And besides, if this was our only chance in a studio, I wanted to get at least one new song put together.

Just for the thrill of it, really. Hearing a song come together, there was nothing like that. Besides, this might be our only chance, and I couldn't help but feel that the songs we had written before, even the ones that hadn't been written all that long ago, were in some ways juvenile. So much had happened since we had first gotten together as a band.

Things were different now than I had ever imagined they would be for us.

As if on cue, I looked over at the bar in time to see Carter polish off another shot. I felt bitterness tighten the corners of my mouth. "You know we'll never be able to pull it off," I said to Luke.

He was silent, and I knew he was thinking of the possibilities as well. What could we do—how could we get out of this situation? Neither of us wanted to ditch Mark and Carter, even if that was the only way to save the band.

Luke laughed bitterly. "I guess it was worth a thought, anyway," he said.

The bitterness in his voice hit me hard. Even though I had spent weeks knowing that the band was falling apart, I didn't want to face the fact that he knew it too.

"I'm not ruling it out," I said fiercely. "But we're going to need to have a serious band meeting first."

"Sure," Luke said, and I could hear from his doubtful tone that he didn't think it would ever happen. That only made me more determined to figure something out, however.

Somehow, I was going to have to get Mark and Carter to get their shit together and focus. Without everyone working together, we were going to blow our shot at stardom, yet I knew that none of us could make it on our own.

For the first time in a while, I felt certain that we had to keep the band together, at any cost.

I looked back toward the bar, though, wondering what that cost might prove to be.

14

LEAH

He was drumming again. He had been so great for the past couple of weeks, practically tiptoeing on eggshells when he knew I was at home, but now he was drumming again. I let out a huff as I looked at my clock. It was nearly two in the morning. What the hell was his problem?

I lay in bed for a moment wondering if I could ignore it. It was unacceptable, but on the other hand, I had been laying low since our hookup. I wasn't sure I had it in me to storm over there, not right now. Who knew what might happen?

I felt a shiver go through me as I considered it.

I thought about the lingerie I had let Piper convince me to buy. It was wrapped in tissue paper in the bottom drawer of my nightstand. Not that I would ever wear it. It was tamer than what my coworker had wanted me to get, but it still wasn't anything I would ever be comfortable in. Even if I agreed that I did look good in it.

What if I went over there now? Dressed in that? But no, I couldn't do that. I just couldn't.

I didn't know what I was waiting for. After talking with Piper, I had been so sure that this was what I wanted. Or rather, I at least wanted to see where things might go with him.

I guess I'd been waiting for some sign from him, though. I didn't expect him to chase me, but I had thought I would, I don't know, hear something from him. I had gone over there with a pizza, after all. He could return the favor, invent some sort of excuse. I didn't have to make all the moves, did I?

I didn't think I was capable of making all the moves. That just wasn't like me.

So when he didn't come after me, I didn't know what to do. Finally, I'd realized that if I wanted something to happen, I was going to have to make a move. I'd put on the lingerie under my robe, hoping to surprise him, and I'd waited and waited for him to come home.

It had been late when he finally did, and I had tried not to feel too worried about it. It didn't mean he had been with a girl, it just meant that his band had something going on that night. That was all.

When he did come home, though, it was with the singer of the band. And on the singer's arms were two beautiful women. I had felt my heart clench in my chest. One of those girls was there for Jayson. I was sure of it.

I felt like such a fool. He was a rock star. Girls were constantly throwing themselves at him. Girls would *continue* to constantly throw themselves at him. He was only going to get more popular. His fame was only going to get greater.

Piper had had all the right words, but she had been

wrong when she said that I could have him, that I was better than those other girls. I had been right. It had been just a one-night thing to him. He didn't care if I had a brain or not. In fact, it was probably better, in his eyes, if I didn't have a brain.

I rolled over, pulling a pillow over my head. It didn't block out the sound of his drumming, though.

I remembered what he had said before, about how drumming was a release for him. I wished I could find some release, but as far as my brain was concerned, the only release I might find that night would be through sex with him, and that wasn't going to happen.

I kept telling myself that if I could just ignore him for long enough, then maybe my crush on him would go away. Instead, it only seemed to get worse, and it was proving impossible to really avoid him when we shared a wall.

In any case, it wasn't as though I could avoid him any longer. Not when things were like this. I wasn't going to march over there in lingerie, but neither was I going to let him keep me up all night as he banged away on his drums. Not when I had an important meeting in the morning. No way. I needed to get some sleep.

I climbed out of bed, cussing all the while. How was it possible that I *wanted* the guy, when he was such an ass? He had absolutely no regard for anyone other than himself. Clearly. I didn't care what sort of personal trouble he was going through at the moment, what sort of things he was working through. You just didn't start slamming on drums in the middle of the night.

I pulled on my robe, wondering as I did so whether I shouldn't put on something a bit more substantial. I remembered the way he had leered at me that first time I went over there. What exactly was I looking for?

I told myself that the only reason I didn't change was because I shouldn't have to get fully dressed and march over there in the middle of the night. I wasn't sure if that was the full truth, though. Nor did I want to examine any of that too closely. He was an ass, and I didn't want to believe he was anything other, or that I couldn't possibly hold myself back, knowing he was an ass.

I banged on his door. When Jayson answered, his face was stormy. As though *he* had a right to be upset. As though *he* was the one who was being kept up in the middle of the night by a rude neighbor.

I gathered myself to yell at him, but something in his expression gave me pause. He was clearly upset about something, and I could tell from the way he was avoiding looking at me, from the way his hands were jammed in his pockets, that it had nothing to do with my knocking on the door.

I thought back to what he had said before, about how drumming was his means of coping. As pissed off as I was at being kept awake before my meeting the next morning, I felt a little flicker of concern go through me. He had been so good about keeping things down since I had told him off the first time; something led me to believe that he wouldn't have broken that pact if there wasn't a damned good reason for it.

Still, where did we go from here? I couldn't sleep if he continued this racket, but something told me he wouldn't be able to sleep if I didn't let him work this out of his system somehow.

Maybe he just needed some other sort of outlet? Venting could help a person out, couldn't it?

"What's wrong?" I asked him.

Jayson's jaw worked for a moment, like he was grinding the words between his teeth rather than spitting them out. As it turned out, though, he had another idea for an outlet, one that had nothing to do with venting. He pulled me into his apartment and into his arms, kicking the door shut behind me.

I went willingly, letting him push me back against the door, his body pressed against mine, his hands frantic as he kissed me deeply.

There was a part of me that knew I should tell him to stop. What, we ignored one another for a couple of weeks, and now suddenly we were going to have sex again? This wasn't the kind of relationship I wanted with anyone. Besides, I had come over here with the idea that I needed to get some sleep at some point tonight.

But I couldn't help melting as he continued to kiss me. It was too hot, too passionate, too much for me to want to hold myself back from him. I started to forget the reasons I had had for wanting to deny this in the first place.

Maybe Piper had been right when she said I could have him if I wanted him. Or was it just that I was the only one here now?

In any case, I would take what I got. I wanted this too badly to do otherwise. Besides, I could tell he needed it. His hands yanked my robe open, stroking my breasts, and I kissed him back, leaning into him, letting him have me.

Maybe there was a way we could both sleep that night.

15

JAYSON

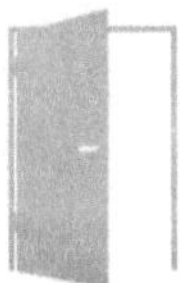

I didn't know what the hell I was doing. I hadn't started drumming with the intention of getting Leah over there, that was for sure. I mean, there was definitely a part of me that felt guilty. I had known when I picked up my sticks that she was probably sleeping just beyond that wall. I had been worried I might wake her up. I just hadn't known what else to do. I needed this.

I didn't even know what *this* was now, though. I had thought I needed to get all my pent-up frustration and worry out in a good bout of drumming. It had been a long night, and I just needed to forget about it.

But kissing Leah seemed to bring me to an even better place. With her pressed up against the door, her robe open and her body on full display, all rational thought evaporated. My focus narrowed down to her and her pleasure—and my own rapidly increasing desire.

I was glad for the rug I had thrown down in the hall at the insistence of an ex-fling of mine. I had never given the thing that much thought after she bought it for me, but now as I bore Leah down on it, unable to make the steps that would take us to the bed or at least the couch, I wondered vaguely if that was the whole reason Brittney had insisted on the rug.

There had never been anyone who made me feel so desperately needy as Leah did. There had never been anyone I felt like I had to have right then and there on the floor.

That was something I didn't want to examine right now, though. I didn't want to think about the consequences of anything. I didn't want to think about addictions or failures or heartaches or anything else. I just wanted to focus on her.

I kissed Leah until she was breathless, her body arching into each caress, small mewls falling from her lips as I teased my fingers across the damp crotch of her panties. She ran her hands down my body, clinging to my ass and pushing up against me with the same desperate need.

I eased her panties out of the way, but I wasn't ready for it to be over just yet. I pushed my fingers inside of her, stroking her walls, making her gasp. Already, her pussy was quaking with the force of her pleasure.

I swiped my thumb across her clit, savoring the sound she made, halfway between a sob and a surprised gasp. I was rock-hard, ready to be inside her... but still, I held back, wanting to be clear-headed as I watched her fall apart.

And God, what a sight it was to see her come undone for me, her legs and mouth falling open on a ragged moan, her arms tossed akimbo into the space above her head as she arched, shuddered, and finally went slack against the rug, that rug that I had never realized the purpose of before.

I knew the purpose of the thing now. I would never be able to forget it, the image of her coming spread out on the floor. It was a promise that she needed the release as badly as I did. I had never seen anything as sexy in my life.

With that thought in mind, I slammed into her, plunging deep. I couldn't have held back for another second, not even with a gun to my head.

I thrust into her sending her over the brink for a second time, and feeling her walls clench and squeeze around me, there was nothing I could do to hold myself back again.

I spilled my slick seed inside of her, crashing through pleasure that thrummed like a cymbal after a hard hit from a mallet.

We collapsed, and even though we were sprawled in the middle of the hall, it was a long time before either of us moved. When it did happen, it was Leah who shifted, and all she did was move closer to me, pressing her body to mine. I wrapped my arms around her, lightly stroking my fingers down her spine, feeling her shiver against me, the aftershocks of pleasure still shaking her to the core. Maybe I was imagining it, but I thought I could still feel her heartbeat moving her entire body.

She sighed happily, nuzzling my chest. I couldn't deny how good it felt to hold her close like that. I looked down at her, and she looked back at me. Slowly, she reached out and tenderly stroked my cheek.

It made something inside of me break open, and all the worries and frustrations started spilling out.

"My band's in trouble," I told her. "We're so close to making it. It's everything we've ever worked for and everything I've ever wanted. But it seems like either the other guys don't want it as badly as I do or, I don't know, maybe they never did. Or maybe they're just not cut out for it."

I paused, and there was a part of me that expected her to pull away. But she didn't. Nor did she say anything—she just lay there staring patiently up at me, waiting for me to continue.

"It's so fucked-up," I exploded. "Mark is too busy fucking groupies to give a shit about anything, and Carter is too drunk to play half the time. He can barely make it through a show most nights. Like, what the hell are we going to do? We have a chance to get signed, there's a guy who might actually be interested in our stuff—and he's only heard our shitty demo that was recorded in a basement. But we're going to blow our chance if we can't pull it together."

Even though talking about it didn't solve anything, I had to admit it felt good to finally say these things. Even though Luke and I were both thinking along the same lines, he didn't want to talk about it. And there was no talking to Carter or Mark. They weren't interested in listening.

Leah listened. She stared attentively up at me, her face screwed up in concentration.

That was the moment when I wondered if I had let things go too far with her. No way was I starting to fall for her. I barely knew her in the first place. Then again, what I knew about her, I liked. She was a gorgeous, kind, thoughtful, smart woman. She wasn't full of herself. She knew what she wanted, and she went for it. She was funny and charming and beautiful, all bundled up in one.

Not to mention, the sex was damn good.

I felt good when I was around her, that was what it really came down to. It almost felt like when I was on stage. There was something about her that made my insides glow. Something about being with her that just felt right somehow.

Finally, Leah spoke. "Sounds like your bandmates are already living like rock stars," she said wryly, giving me a crooked smile. "Have you tried reminding them how precarious their position is? How fleeting fame can be if they don't put the work in? Maybe that would push them to get back in the studio."

My mouth twisted in frustration. Her words made sense, and I wished I believed words like that might make a difference. "I don't think they'd get that," I sighed. "They're so focused on sex, booze, and who knows what else that they just don't have the bandwidth to conceptualize that."

"Sure," Leah said, shrugging. "You know, when I was a math tutor, I realized that I needed to put things into terms that my students could understand. Deal with things that they had actually experienced. A lot of times, I'd remind them that if they failed, they'd only have to take the class over again, which meant prolonging the torture."

I understood what she was saying, but not quite what she was getting at. "Maybe it's not so much the threat of losing it or never getting it—maybe it's the reminder that otherwise they're going to have to go back to the way things were before you got big," she said.

I blinked down at her. "That's not a bad idea," I said slowly. Then, I shook my head. "I'm not sure they're listening, though."

Leah grinned at me. "You weren't much interested in listening to me about the drumming, either, until I threatened to go to the landlord," she reminded me.

I snorted, unable to help my amusement. I felt even more guilty at having disturbed her that night, even if I was happy with the way things had ended, with her here in my arms.

"Maybe I should have you talk to them," I suggested teasingly. "You could put the fear of God in them."

Leah laughed, and there was something so sweet and pure about the sound that I couldn't help but kiss her again.

She allowed me to for a moment, then slowly detangled herself from me. "I need to get some sleep," she said, getting to her feet and grabbing her discarded robe.

I felt disappointment boil inside of me. I could tell that she didn't mean to stay there. Still, I couldn't help but mention, "My bed is just this way."

Leah shook her head, but there was a fleeting look of regret on her face. "I can't," she said gently. She cleared her throat. "I have a meeting early tomorrow morning, and I really need to be rested for it."

I wondered if it was another excuse, if she was just trying to get away from me like she had the last time. I guess it didn't really matter either way. The point was, she wasn't staying.

I was disappointed by that. I couldn't remember ever being so invested in sleeping arrangements before. Still, I forced myself to get slowly to my feet. There was a part of me that was kicking myself. Maybe if I hadn't fucked her right there in the hallway, maybe if I had taken her to the bedroom like the prized catch that she was, then she wouldn't feel like this was nothing more than a quick fling.

Maybe she would have felt like she could stay.

In any case, it was too late for those regrets now. She was re-robed, smiling gently up at me. She stood on her tiptoes and gave me one last kiss, but this one was quick and emotionless. "See ya," she said. Then, she headed back to her place, leaving me alone in my front hall.

I headed into the living room, looking longingly at my drums. But no. As much as I wanted to summon her back over here, I wouldn't do that to her. She had said that she had a meeting in the morning. I could only imagine how pissed she would be if I kept her up all night.

Besides, I didn't really feel all that much like drumming

anymore. I felt quietly restless, but it didn't feel like drumming could fix things. I needed to do something productive. Something like talking to my bandmates.

There was nothing I could do right now, though. I headed into my room and climbed into bed. In spite of the earlier exertion, it was a long time before I fell asleep.

LEAH

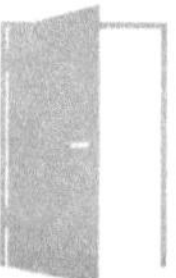

I looked around the bar, trying not to feel out of place. I was in a dim booth with Piper, and Jayson's band was about to play. I had been excited when Piper suggested we go to the show. I had looked up the band's gig schedule on their social media pages, but I hadn't wanted to go alone. Still, I hadn't felt comfortable asking Piper if she wanted to go with me, not after I had told her about sleeping with Jayson.

I hadn't told her about the second incident, the one that had involved him fucking me right there in the middle of the hallway. I still got shivers thinking back to it, but I couldn't help wondering if maybe I should have felt ashamed of myself.

Who was I, anyway? How had I gone from someone who never had one-night stands to someone who let someone fuck them on the floor as though... Well, as though I was just some needy groupie.

I didn't know how to talk to Piper about all of it, the

crisis of confidence in who I was. I couldn't help but wonder if maybe coming to LA had been a mistake, but since I had only moved to LA because of the job and because Piper was my coworker at said job, I knew that telling her about it all could complicate things.

In any case, when she had asked if I wanted to go see the band play that night, I had been secretly relieved, in spite of how nervous I'd been. Yet it hadn't taken two minutes of being there before I regretted letting her drag me along.

It had definitely been a mistake, that much was clear. I didn't want to watch him flirt with groupies, but already there was a crowd gathered around the stage, most of them thin, young, sexy women.

My mouth twisted as I watched one blonde in particular. She was standing off to the side of the stage, chatting with Jayson as he finished setting up his things for the show. I hated her immediately, and I didn't even know her. Still, I could tell from the way she smiled at him and flipped her hair back that she wanted him.

I didn't want anyone else to have him.

I wondered where the jealousy was coming from. I wasn't sure I had ever felt that way before. Did it mean I had feelings for him? What was I going to do about it if so?

Piper rapped her fingers on the table in between us. "Those girls have nothing on you," she said seriously as I turned back to her. I gave my friend a smile, even if I didn't feel the same sense of assurance. Surely if Jayson didn't want the attention, if he wasn't interested in her, then he would have shut her down by now?

My thoughts were thankfully interrupted by the sound of the band beginning their show, Mark starting to talk to the crowd through the mic and Carter starting to strum a few aimless and wandering chords.

It wasn't just coincidental that my jealousy subsided as the blonde girl fell back with a small frown on her face, Jayson clearly having said something to disappoint her.

The band was every bit as good as they had been the previous time I had seen them, but in light of what Jayson had told me the night we had slept together on his rug, I couldn't help watching everyone a little more closely than before. I could see signs of the undercurrents he had mentioned. I could see that Mark flirted with the crowd with more relish than he seemed to put into any of their songs. I could see Carter's small stumble that nearly took him off the stage in the middle of a particularly tricky solo.

They were talented, and I knew I wouldn't have picked up on it if I hadn't known to look for it. At the same time, it was only a matter of time before things went too far, before it all boiled over.

I hoped for Jayson's sake that that wouldn't happen. I hoped that the guys could get it together for long enough to hit the big time.

As the show went on, I started getting into the music as did everyone else. The girls at the front of the stage were all dancing seductively, drawing the attention of the band. Mark was only encouraging them. My jealousy flared up again. How could I possibly hope to hold Jayson's attention in light of all of that? I didn't even know how to play the game.

Fortunately, Piper seemed to realize just what I was thinking. "Come on," she said, suddenly grabbing my hands and dragging me out to the dance floor. "I know how to deal with girls like that," she breathed into my ear. She gave me a wicked smile as she pulled back a little, her hands catching my hips and moving me along with her.

She danced with me, and I tried my best to keep up with her, to match her move for seductive move. I knew that I probably looked stiff and awkward, like I had no idea what I was doing. At least at first. But then the music took over, pounding through me, and I let myself go. It wasn't long before I spun away from Piper. When I turned toward the stage, Jayson's cautious attention was trained on me.

I smirked at him, doing everything in my power to make him lose his concentration as I swung my hips to the beat. He didn't mess up, but from the smoldering heat in his gaze, as well as the way his eyes never left me, I knew I was having an effect on him.

Maybe Piper was right. Maybe I could have him if I really wanted him. The thought sent a thrill through me.

The set eventually came to an end, and the crowd erupted with noise. I grinned ruefully at Piper as she gave me an "I told you so" look. "I guess I owe you a drink," I shouted above the applause.

Piper laughed and we headed toward the bar. I glanced back over my shoulder, but Jayson was already preoccupied in breaking things down. Still, it was only a matter of time before he found me.

I didn't want to speculate on where the evening might end, but I had a good feeling we might end up in bed again, if nothing else. Even though I still had some reservations about the whole thing, I had to admit I wanted him.

We waited at the bar to get the bartender's attention. It seemed like everyone else had the same idea as us, needing a refresher as soon as the set was over. I supposed that was a good sign for the band. Everyone had been so engrossed in the music that empty glasses had gone unheeded until now. They really were that good.

Someone suddenly dropped their arm around my shoulders, and I smiled. I turned, expecting to see Jayson there. Instead, it was the singer, Mark. He leered at me. "You know, I couldn't keep my eyes off you the whole set," he said. "Do you have any idea what you do to a man?"

I blinked up at him, still trying to process. Yet again, I felt like I just didn't know the rules of the game. Was this a thing? Jayson thought he could just sleep with me and then tell his bandmates that I was easy and they could have at me?

But no. As soon as the thought crossed my mind, I knew he would never have done that. I remembered how roughly he'd pulled Carter off of me a few weeks before. Except that didn't change the fact that Mark seemed to think he had some right to put his hands all over me.

He leaned in close, practically nuzzling my neck. "I don't do this very often, but how would you and your friend like to come back to my place?"

I rolled my eyes, shrugging my way out from beneath his arm. Out of the corner of my eye, I noticed Jayson headed toward us. The look on his face was murderous and it sent a little thrill through me. Maybe I wasn't the only one that had caught feelings.

Still, I tried to downplay the situation so as not to cause greater turmoil than there already was within the band.

"Sorry, I'm not interested," I said.

"Oh come on," Mark wheedled, apparently oblivious to the approach of Jayson's wrath. "Who are you saving it for? Does he know what a cocktease you are?"

I scowled, unable to help bristling at his words. "As a matter of fact, I'm only interested in dating guys who have a shot at making it big, not some lazy hack singer from a local band."

Mark looked confused at that, but before he had really had a chance to react, Jayson was there, grabbing him by the collar and yanking him away from me.

JAYSON

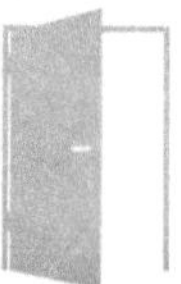

I was about to lose it. As if the set hadn't been terrible enough. Now, on top of that disappointment of an evening, I had to watch Mark try and flirt with Leah? That was just too much.

I didn't know which of the three of us I was more pissed at, and that bothered me more than anything else could have. Was it Mark for always having to flirt with another girl, and another, and another, until it seemed like there was no one left in the whole city he hadn't had his paws on? Was it Leah for allowing him to sling an arm around her shoulders like that?

Or was I just mad at myself for not staking my claim to her before someone else gave it a try?

The thing was, I knew I couldn't be mad at Mark. I had never really cared before about who he hit on; I just cared that his insistence on hitting on girls at the moment seemed to be interfering with his ability to be the singer in our band.

No, it wasn't Mark I was mad at.

I couldn't be mad at Leah, either. As she slipped away from Mark and turned to look at him with fury in her eyes, I could tell that none of it had been her idea. She didn't welcome his advances, and she certainly hadn't invited them.

That made relief go through me. Even if it meant that the only person I had left to be mad at was myself. Leah was different. Leah was all mine.

I yanked Mark away from her, causing him to let out a little yelp of surprise. But before I could give him what for, Leah was laying into him.

"You might have a bunch of groupies now, but do you really think you're still going to be relevant in a year if your band is just playing the same old songs in the same old smelly bars?" she snapped, folding her arms across her chest and giving him an unimpressed look. "No, you won't be. That's not how it works. You either get your shit together or there will be someone new and exciting, and you'll be forgotten about."

The words made me wince. It was everything I had been thinking for weeks now. All my worst nightmares, just what I dreaded was our band's fate. Voiced out loud, in her scornful tone, I couldn't help but want to go home to bed and pull the covers over my head for the rest of forever.

She was right. We were never going to amount to anything. If she knew it, all our other fans were bound to realize it sooner or later. There was nothing for it; might as well give up now.

Except that I'd always been stubborn when it came to something I really wanted, and Leah was proving to be as well.

"Yeah, I thought that might shut you up," she said. "But just shutting up isn't good enough. I hope you remember this in the morning, and I hope you pull your shit together. Because otherwise, it's only a matter of time before you're a washed-up nobody with no options."

I could see Mark physically deflate before my eyes. I released him, trying not to laugh at the expression on his face. I couldn't help but feel impressed by Leah. She certainly had a knack for getting people to do what she wanted them to do. I only hoped that where Mark was concerned, the truth spurred him into action rather than making him just give up like I'd momentarily wanted to do.

Mark didn't seem to know what to say. Finally, he just turned and stalked off. I was surprised to see him brush off some of the groupies who flocked to his side. In fact, he walked clear out of the bar. He might just be going to smoke and cool down, but I hoped he might head home and actually get some sleep for once.

"What's gotten into him?" Luke asked quizzically, joining us at just the moment that Mark left.

I shrugged, still eyeing Leah. "I guess he finally met a fan who didn't melt when he looked in her direction," I finally said.

"Huh," Luke said, looking at first Leah and then Piper. He did a double-take, looking back at Piper, and I could see Leah's friend blush and duck her head.

"Listen, we're going to go get some air and talk about some things," I told Luke, making a split-second decision that whatever the future might hold for us, I needed them all to know that Leah was mine. "Can you chat with..." I trailed off, realizing I didn't know Leah's friend's name.

"Piper," she supplied, smiling coyly at Luke.

"Sure," Luke said, not looking back at me as I all but dragged Leah away.

I thought Leah might protest, but when I turned to face

her backstage in the warm-up room, she looked like the cat that ate the canary. "Were you jealous, back there?" she asked.

I rolled my eyes. "Of course not," I muttered. But I couldn't help but say, "First Carter, then me, now Mark, though? You trying to work your way through the band?"

It was a reflection of my earlier anger coming back. Even though I knew that wasn't the way things were with her, there was a part of me that couldn't forget that I barely knew her. Who knew what she was really all about?

Leah didn't look angry, to my surprise. Anger was what I would have expected from her. Instead, she just looked sad and hurt. "You should realize by now that I'm not like that," she said. "I'm not just some groupie." She smiled wryly. "To be honest, a lot of my problems would be solved if you weren't a drummer."

I snorted with amusement. "I know," I sighed. Then, plainly: "I didn't like turning around and seeing his arm around you like that. No more than I liked seeing Carter get close to you."

I never said the word "jealous," but it was there in all of it. How would she take that? What did I *mean* by that?

For a moment, I let myself picture what it would be like to have a relationship with her. It was hard to imagine her wanting such a thing, though. She was a good girl, and I was the drummer in some local band. She had a career. We might both be focused on the future, we might both be driven, but that was where the similarities ended.

This wasn't going anywhere. It couldn't.

Did I want it to? I cared about her; I knew that. I couldn't seem to get her out of my head, either. Maybe I did want something more with her. I knew it would be a doomed relationship, though.

It wouldn't be worth going down that road just for both of us to get hurt in the end.

Fortunately, Leah didn't press me for more. She didn't tease me for my jealousy. She simply nodded once, slowly. There was something serious and calculating in her gaze, and I wondered if she was thinking along the same lines as me. I wondered if she had come to the same conclusions as me.

Suddenly, I couldn't stand the distance between us. Who knew how long things would last? Who knew how long the window of opportunity would be there? I had to take advantage of it while I could.

I kissed her hard and long, my body still buzzing with adrenaline from the show and from the anger of seeing Mark with his arm around her. For her part, Leah kissed back just as ferociously, her lips jammed up against mine, her tongue a furious presence in my mouth. It was raw and just this side of painful, and somehow it was just another side of the sexiness that she always seemed to exhibit.

I didn't want to let her go. I definitely didn't want to watch her go back out into that bar where anyone else could see her. I wished there was some way I could let everyone know that she was mine. I had to settle with kissing her until her lips were swollen, her eyes dark with lust.

I didn't want anyone else to have her. I wanted to be the only one.

I was in over my head, but I didn't know what to do about it. She was my lifeline but at the same time, she was my kryptonite.

I kissed her again, sweeter this time. As she slowly smiled up at me, I had a flash of clarity. I knew I was hooked and that there was no going back.

LEAH

My heart was pounding, just like it always seemed to be when Jayson was near. I had to admit, the whole evening had been thrilling in ways I had never experienced before. From dancing, watching Jayson up on the stage, to standing at the bar yelling at Mark, to being dragged back here, it was as though every small detail of each moment was seared into my brain.

Jayson seemed to hold the key to all the extremes of sensory pleasure for me. I had never felt like this before, and I knew inexplicably that I would never feel this way about anyone else for the rest of my life.

No, Jayson was special to me. And somehow, I knew that I was special to him as well.

That first kiss had my toes curling in my shoes. There was so much emotion in there, so much tension. I wanted him to drag me over to one of the questionable-looking couches along the back wall and take me right there, where anyone could walk in and see us.

This wasn't me. Or this wasn't a side of myself that I had ever known before. I wanted to feel ashamed of the way I gave in to him, but there was something about it all that was just so thrilling at the same time. And really, why should I be ashamed? We were two adults, and we wanted one another. We hadn't talked about the terms of a relationship, but he clearly didn't want to see me with anyone else, and that was good enough for now, wasn't it?

He was a rock star, and he'd had had plenty of chances to bring someone else back here tonight, or even to watch someone else dancing around in front of the stage, but instead, he'd only had eyes for me. That was as good as anything that I could expect.

I was starting to wonder if maybe I had been too hasty in my judgment of him. Maybe we could make it work after all.

I shivered, my thoughts derailing as Jayson kissed his way along the tender skin of my neck. "You have no idea how turned on I was watching you dance," he said, but as he rubbed up against me, I could feel just how hard he was, his bulge practically ripping a hole in his jeans. I reached down and stroked the fabric, and he groaned against my skin, his hips bucking toward me.

Things got hot and messy after that, our kisses turning sloppy, our hands groping and grasping. My whole body prickled with lust, and my chest swelled with emotions I didn't dare name just yet.

Before things could go too far, though, the door opened. I yanked away from Jayson feeling embarrassed as well as annoyed at the interruption. Was it so much to ask that we could...

My thoughts trailed off at the look on Luke's face. He looked genuinely apologetic as he averted his eyes from us.

"Hey, man, sorry to interrupt, but I need a hand with Carter. I wouldn't ask if he wasn't making a total ass of himself."

Jayson sighed and ran a hand back through his hair. For a moment, I could tell it was on the tip of his tongue to tell Luke to deal with it himself. But then he tucked himself back in and zipped up his pants, giving me an apologetic look. "Sure thing," he said, heading toward the door. "What's he up to now?"

I tried not to feel too disappointed as he walked out of there without saying another word to me. I knew how important the band was to him. I shouldn't feel slighted. They had to come first. Still, standing there alone in the backroom, straightening my clothing and feeling the dampness between my thighs, I couldn't help but feel cheap.

If I was going to have Jayson, I wanted him to lay me down on soft sheets, to take his time with me. I wanted to lie together all night, his arms around me, his body warm against mine. I wanted soft caresses and sweet kisses.

I wanted the promise of something more. That was what I was really missing here, and what I was really craving. Standing there alone in the backroom, I knew that things were no more resolved than they had ever been. We hadn't talked about the terms of a relationship. There was no *relationship*. He was just a guy I had slept with a few times.

I took a deep breath and let it out slowly, trying not to feel disappointed with it all. I remembered what Piper had told me: if I wanted him, I could have him. I had something that the rest of the groupies didn't have.

I had felt that way earlier in the night, anyway. I tried to cling to that feeling now.

I headed out into the bar, pasting a smile on my face. I

knew that if Jayson was dealing with Carter, it was probably going to be an all-night thing with Carter crashing at his place again. I tried to tell myself that that was fine. There would be another time.

In any case, it sounded like Luke was involved in things too, which meant that Piper probably wasn't getting anything more out of him that night, either. We would head home and do this again another night. No big deal.

As I was on my way back to Piper, though, a cute bottle-blonde stepped into my path. "Hey, new girl," she said in a way that was anything but friendly or welcoming. "Listen, I know you don't know how things work around here, but there's a bit of a hierarchy where it comes to us. I've got dibs on Jayson."

I blinked at her, barely believing the words had just come out of her mouth. She had dibs on him? Like he was just some toy for them to squabble over. I made a face of disgust. Who *was* this chick?

"I think that's up to Jayson to decide," I said.

The woman narrowed her eyes at me. "You might be having fun with him now, but you know it won't last," she said coolly.

I rolled my eyes. "You have no idea what Jayson and I have, so why don't you just butt out?"

She loomed closer. "I've seen a lot of bands, and I've never seen a musician be faithful for long. That's not the kind of thing that a girl like you is looking for, and we both know it. So why don't you leave him for someone who can handle him?"

I bristled, but before I could say anything else, she turned and sauntered away toward the bar, not giving me a backward glance.

I frowned. I didn't want to believe what she had said to

me, but on the other hand, she had given voice to some of the same fears I'd had about Jayson from the start.

And hell, I had seen him come home with Mark and those two girls, hadn't I? I didn't even know if he had been faithful since the first time we had slept together, and that had only been a matter of weeks. Granted, we had never outright talked about fidelity. How could I ever expect it from him, though?

They weren't even famous yet. They might be a big enough thing to keep playing shows and to have a coterie that followed them from bar to bar, but they weren't a huge sensation like they could potentially be if they pulled it together and were heard by the right people.

How could I compete against all the other women who would throw themselves at him once he really made it? I just couldn't do that.

It wasn't that I lacked self-esteem, I was just realistic. I was some girl from a small town in the middle of nowhere. My life had been somewhat sheltered, now that I thought about it, and I knew that I lacked a certain sophistication and worldliness. I was destined to wind up with someone quiet and gentle and small-town just like me. That was just the way things worked.

In any case, I had to admit that there was a reason we had never discussed the relationship thing, or even discussed whether this fling was a thing that would continue. It wasn't just that we could barely be in the same room with one another without ripping off one another's clothes. No, the real reason was that I knew exactly how that conversation would go.

Even if he promised to try to be faithful to me, there was no way I could expect him to uphold that end of the bargain. Just like I couldn't trust him not to wake me up in the middle of the night with his drumming. It was just the person he was, and there was no changing that.

I didn't have any right to *try* to change that.

No, that groupie was right. He would be better off with someone who could handle the lifestyle that he lived. That person wasn't me. I had surprised myself with everything I had done since I had come to LA, but there were certain things that would never change about me. I would never be with someone I couldn't trust to be faithful to me. That was all there was to it.

I couldn't help but feel a little depressed as I headed back to where I had left Piper before.

"Are you okay?" Piper asked immediately, seeing the expression on my face. I didn't want to talk about it, though, so I waved the question away.

"I've got early meetings tomorrow," I told her. "I think it's probably time to call it a night and head home."

Piper frowned. "Do you want to at least wait for Jayson?" she asked. "Sounds like they're just going to stuff the guitarist in a car; I'm sure it won't take long." I could hear from the hopeful note in her voice that she was hoping I would stick around so that she would have a reason to hang around waiting for Luke.

I just wanted to go home and forget that tonight had happened. I couldn't seem to get the blonde's words out of my head. This thing that Jayson and I had, there was no way it could last.

I still didn't know the rules of the game, but all the other players did. Not only that, but I was sure they knew how to take advantage of the rules to make sure I could never win.

Best to forget about all of it, put my head down, and focus on my career like I'd intended to when I'd moved out here. No matter how much I wished I was still in that back room with Jayson, with his hands playing across my skin.

"Even after they're done dealing with Carter, they're going to have to break down the whole stage and everything," I pointed out. "That's going to take a while."

Piper frowned for a moment, but something about her expression told me that she knew exactly what I wasn't saying. She looked sympathetic. I looked away from her, not wanting to see any of that.

"You can stay if you want," I said, shrugging one shoulder. I faked a yawn. "But I think I need to get home. Sorry. This has been fun, but I'm still kind of a grandma."

Piper laughed and shook her head. "Come on, let's go, then. We'll catch them another night."

"Sure," I said, even though I knew I couldn't let myself keep doing this.

I wasn't one of their groupies. I never would be. That was the whole problem.

It felt like each time I saw Jayson, I got more and more entangled with him. We were getting closer, and I was losing my heart to him. But that was such a huge risk. I couldn't handle dating a musician who was trying to break into the big time. This just wasn't my scene—the long nights, the parties, the women.

That wasn't the kind of lifestyle I could realistically be a part of.

I looked around the bar one last time on the way out. No one was looking at me, but I couldn't shake the feeling that they were all judging me somehow. Like that blonde groupie, they all knew I didn't belong.

I wished I could talk to Piper about it, but I didn't know how to tell her what I was feeling without betraying just how much of a country bumpkin I was.

Instead, I kept my thoughts inside and later spent the night tossing and turning, I kept thinking of what it would be like to start a relationship, but then eventually, I would come around to remembering that I couldn't be with him. I didn't know why I couldn't seem to get him out of my mind.

I didn't know why I was so disappointed when I didn't hear him come home.

JAYSON

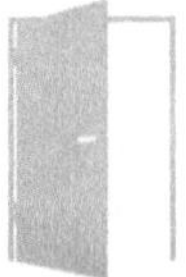

I listened to the guitar die away into silence. For a moment, none of us said anything. Then, Mark threw a fist in the air, letting out a little whoop. "That might be perfect," he said, grinning ear to ear as he turned toward me.

I nodded. "That was pretty good," I said cautiously. But I couldn't help grinning as well. "Better than pretty good, I guess," I corrected. "We might be able to put that one on the album."

It had been a few weeks, and we were in the studio. To be honest, I hadn't expected that this would ever happen. And even if it did ever happen, I hadn't held out any hope that things would actually work out this well.

Something about Leah yelling at Mark in the middle of the bar seemed to have struck a nerve. He still liked to chase after women whenever he had a chance, which was pretty frequently considering that we were only in the studio for a limited amount of time each day. At the same time, he was really putting some effort in, in a way that I hadn't expected from him for a while now.

It wasn't just him, either. Once Mark started to put himself back together, Carter had seemed to take a cue. Or maybe it was just the fact that the rest of us sat him down and told him that if he didn't chill out with the drinking while we were in the studio, then we were going to find someone to replace him with.

Mark had actually led that charge. I still credited it all to Leah's intervention, though.

Working on new songs, putting together some different tunes, felt amazing. I had forgotten how good it felt to hear something come to life, to be honest. It was creating life; it was furthering our dreams.

Not only that, but the things we were putting together now, these new songs, were our best work yet. By far. I couldn't wait to show them to the world. The first person I wanted to have hear them outside of us, though, was Leah. It was all because of her.

It wasn't just that she had gotten my bandmates to shape up and put the work in; it was also that she had inspired me to push myself as well. She really seemed to believe in us. She really seemed to think we could make it. But in order to do that, we were all going to have to work harder, myself included.

The lyrics I had put together for the new songs were way better than anything I had put together before. They felt relevant. They felt like the kind of songs people would resonate with. They felt like the kind of songs we wouldn't regret if we were still singing them five or ten years from now.

Somehow, when Carter sobered up some, his guitar playing was better than it had ever been before. I didn't think he had been practicing all that much, but he surprised us, pulling out some new riffs that none of us could possibly have expected. It amped up the pieces, even as it sounded forlorn and haunting. There was a hopeless, transcendent quality to it that worked well with the lyrics I was writing.

We had all come together for this one, and it sure sounded like magic.

This could be our ticket. I felt goosebumps go up my arms as we listened back through parts of it.

Things still weren't finished yet. We were still missing a song or two, and I think we could all feel that. Still, we were getting closer, and I had a feeling that by the time we ran out of time at the studio, we were going to be at least well on our way, if not fully finished. I hadn't felt this excited about anything for a long time now.

Except that there was one thing that had gotten me to this level of excitement, but I hadn't seen Leah since the night she had yelled at Mark, and it was bumming me out. I didn't know how to see her, though. I mean, sure, she lived next door to me, but I didn't know how to approach her.

I didn't know what she was thinking; that's what it really came down to. I had thought that things were going well after the concert she'd been at. Or at least, she certainly hadn't been complaining when we were together in the back room. If Luke hadn't interrupted us, I didn't know where things might have gone.

But he had interrupted us, and by the time I had gotten done with the Carter situation, she was gone. I had thought that she might have just gone to the bathroom or something, and that she might reappear by the time I was done helping Luke tear down the equipment and load it into the van.

But she hadn't come back and she hadn't said goodbye. I wasn't sure how to feel about that.

Of course, I had thought about going over there to thank her for helping us out. She had been a huge part of my personal inspiration, but she had helped to get the rest of them on track too. Not only that, but I still wanted to talk to her about us. That one night had been so therapeutic. It had felt so good to get things out.

She was the only person I wanted to tell everything to, good or bad.

There was something more to that, but I wasn't sure I was ready to start examining it. Especially since I had a feeling that she was avoiding me again.

I had been worried about that before, but then she had shown up at my place. This time, though, nothing seemed to summon her over, not even a 3:00 A.M. drum session.

She didn't want to see me. I had to be okay with that. Besides, she was probably just busy at work. I was busy with my music; I got how that went. Not only that, but I was trying to set a good example for Mark, not chasing tail, and Carter was still crashing at my place most nights. It was just a complicated time.

Still, I missed her. We had a connection; I was sure of it. I missed the way her body felt against mine. I missed the way she listened to me. I missed the way she stood up for what she believed in.

I was falling for her. I was ready to admit that. She was different from anyone I had been with before, and I couldn't get enough of her. That said, I was trying to focus on my work. I had a feeling that that tension was part of why my music was better now than it had ever been before. It was another thing I wanted to tell her, but I was afraid she wouldn't understand it and would think I was nuts.

No, I needed her to listen to our music. But in order for

that to happen, we had to finish up the album. We weren't quite there yet.

"Alright, let's break for the day," I said to everyone.

"Yeah, we've got that show tomorrow," Mark added. "I should rest my voice before that. And Carter, you should rest your fingers."

"Yeah, sure," Carter said, nodding.

We all packed up and headed our separate ways. There was no talk of vices. There were no plans to go out together that night. The truth was, things might be going better for us in terms of the band, but in terms of our personal lives, it felt like we weren't even friends anymore. I knew it was going to take some time to rebuild those bridges, but it didn't feel like anyone was even trying.

It felt like I was working with strangers. Like we might never reconnect again. At least we had a chance to make it again, but I still didn't know if making it was worth the price of our friendship.

It was another thing I wished that I could talk to Leah about. Or even Luke. Instead, I let them all leave and then sat down at the drum set, wailing away for another half hour before I felt okay to go home. On the way, I stopped by one of my favorite bars. It was a place that Carter and Luke and Mark and I all used to frequent together. I guess I was feeling a little bit nostalgic.

When I went inside, I almost smiled to see Carter there. For a moment, I forgot about alcoholism or anything else. For a moment, it felt just like old times as I headed to the bar and sat on a bar seat next to him, flagging down the bartender to order a beer for myself.

Carter clinked his beer against mine, but he didn't say anything still.

"Your playing was really good today," I finally said.

"Like, really good. You've added something to the album that I'm really impressed with actually."

Carter hummed and took a sip of his beer.

I started to babble. "You know, part of what's been influencing my songwriting lately has been Leah. She makes me work harder than I think I ever had before. How you doin' bro?"

To be honest, we were all wondering what it was that had gotten Carter to shape up. I still couldn't believe that it was just the intervention or the fact that Mark had started to pull himself together. I wished that Carter would let me in, that he would trust me enough to let me know what was going on in his life.

Carter's playing was increasingly better, but there was something melancholic about it, a sadness I had never heard before. I wondered where that was coming from, but I hadn't been sure how to ask, prior to now.

I was starting to realize, though, that I had been so absorbed in the band, in making it with them, that it had been a while since I'd really shown any of my friends how much I actually cared about them. Carter had been right to blow me off when I had told him that he needed to shape up. I had mostly been worried about him in terms of how it would affect the band. That wasn't right.

Leah had broadened my focus some. Reminded me that the outside world existed and that it wasn't all down to my drums and our shows.

Carter shrugged, his expression going dark. I could tell that it definitely wasn't a relationship that was informing his playing. He wasn't in love. So what was it?

Whatever it was, Carter didn't let me in on it now. That shrug was apparently all I was going to get out of him. He didn't want to open up. I wondered if whatever it was was the same thing that drove him to drink like he did. If the reason all of it was coming out in his playing now was because he wasn't drinking so much, he wasn't numbing that pain beneath the veneer of alcohol that had kept it hidden before.

I wondered if maybe not drinking wasn't such a good thing if he wasn't going to get help by other means so that he could actually deal with it.

I knew better than to say anything like that, though. He wouldn't welcome it, and it would only make our friendship more tenuous than it already was. Better to take the time and build things up between us again. Eventually, when we were on better terms, maybe he would tell me all about it.

Could we wait, though? I was afraid that if he kept everything all bottled up inside... I didn't want to think about it. But then again, just because he wasn't talking to me about things, it didn't mean that he wasn't talking to anyone. Luke listened better than anyone I knew, and Mark was going through some shit right now too. The likelihood was, Carter just didn't want to talk to *me* about it. That was fine.

Still, I did want to put the work in to build up our friendship again. "Want to hang out tonight?" I asked. "Just kick back and watch some shit on TV or something?"

Carter raised an eyebrow at me. "Didn't you just say something about a girl?" he asked, and the smirk on his face almost reminded me of the old days.

I laughed. "She's out of town," I said, shrugging, remembering her on the sidewalk with her suitcase the day before. "I'm bored as fuck."

Carter snorted. "Sure," he said. "Sounds like fun."

"Just let me hit the head," I told him.

"Sure, meet you out front," Carter said.

I grinned as I headed off to the bathroom. Things were going well with the band, and soon enough, life was going to be back to normal. It was an incredible relief.

I knew I needed to keep my head in the game, not go mooning after Leah. I couldn't afford to screw up or shirk my responsibilities.

I thought about Leah again and wondered why she was avoiding me. Was she really just busy with work and life, or did she realize that she didn't want anything from me? I shook my head and tried to break my train of thought. Maybe she was just waiting for me to make a move. It wasn't like I'd gone after her either. No, I needed to go see her as soon as she got home from wherever it was that she'd gone.

I was glad to have a little time to focus on my relationships with my friends.

Except that when I headed out front, Carter was nowhere to be seen. I even ducked back into the bar, wondering if he was still finishing his beer. But he was gone. My hands clenched into fists. What the fuck, man?

I frowned, heading home alone. I couldn't help but wonder where Carter was. He hadn't been noticeably drunk at the bar, but then again, I wondered if I would even notice if he was buzzed at this point. It was just a relief to see that he wasn't falling all over himself or picking fights. That didn't mean he was *sober*, that just meant that he wasn't three sheets to the wind.

Yet again, I wondered at how blind I could be. Here I had been acting like everything was all better, ignoring all signs to the contrary. I wasn't looking out for Carter at all, just for my own interests and the band. What kind of an ass was I?

I remembered how frustrated Leah had been the first

night she came over to my place, yelling at me to keep it down. She was right—I really was self-absorbed. I didn't care about anyone other than myself. Or if I did, my actions certainly didn't show it.

I thought about Leah again. I wasn't good enough for her, that was for sure. Not even close.

I unlocked my door, my eyes slipping over to her side of the duplex. Even if she had been there, I couldn't go over there and tell her about my band woes. I had done that once already, and she had immediately jumped in and done her best to fix things for me.

It was time for me to start fixing things for myself. If only I knew where to start. At this point, the idea of putting us back together, of getting back to the way it had been before, seemed like an impossible task.

I sighed and flopped down on my couch, staring up at the ceiling.

LEAH

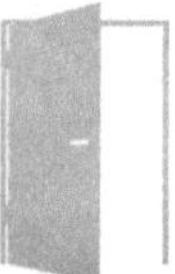

I really hadn't been sure what to expect from the work retreat, but I had to admit, I was really enjoying myself. It was just the accounting team, and I was enjoying the chance to really get a chance to know some of my coworkers outside the office. We were deep in the San Bernardino Forest, in a place that was sort of like a summer camp for grown-ups.

It was a welcome break from the concrete jungle of the city. I hadn't realized how much I was missing open spaces until I got here. It made sense, though; I had never lived in a place like LA before, with its high-rise buildings, traffic, and smog. Getting out into nature, whatever kind it was, felt glorious.

It wasn't just the surroundings, though; the whole atmosphere was great. It was a total change from being in the office every day, but I already felt like we were sure to work more like a team from here on out.

I would happily have stayed for longer if we could.

We only had a few nights there, though. We had come up early on Friday, and we were leaving this afternoon. Most of Friday and Saturday had been spent on team-building activities and brainstorming exercises. There was a large lodge in the midst of all the little cabins which served as home base for us for the weekend.

We had done a little bit of everything. Nothing that had directly related to our work, but all meant to utilize the same skills that we needed to do our jobs. I had to admit, doing trust falls with people who had been my coworkers for such a short time was nerve-wracking. I just had to keep reminding myself that Piper had been at the company for longer than I had and still barely knew some of them.

In any case, I was game for it, and I felt closer to them all now. I was glad that I had come into the company at the time I had.

Now, it was early Sunday morning, and I was sitting out on the front porch of our cabin, sipping at some coffee, listening to birdsong, and waiting for the rest of them to get up. Most of them had stayed up a lot later than I had the night before. I felt like a grandma going to sleep as early as I had, but after staying up so late on Friday night, I wasn't up for a repeat on Saturday, unfortunately.

I had been feeling tired a lot lately. I knew it was just my body getting used to my new schedule and my new environment. Not only that, but it needed to recover for those couple of nights I let Piper keep me out late or Jayson keep me up late.

Besides, today was the day that I needed to put my best foot forward, and I wouldn't be able to do that if I was overtired and cranky. Today was the day for one-on-ones with the people at the company who made the real decisions.

Piper had been preparing for this day for a while now, trying to ensure she got that promotion she wanted.

Even though I was new, making a good impression today could set me up for future success, and I wasn't about to squander that chance.

With that thought in mind, I headed back into the cabin I shared with Piper. She was in the shower at the moment. I turned my attention to considering the outfits I had brought with me. I had definitely overpacked for the weekend, but I didn't regret doing so. I hadn't really known how casual things were going to be, so I'd wanted to bring a few different options. Today was the day to make sure I was dressed to impress.

I knew that Piper was planning to "dress for the job she wanted," and I thought that was pretty solid advice. At the same time, most of our higher-ups had been walking around in jeans and T-shirts for the weekend, and I had a feeling that was likely to be the case today as well. I didn't want to feel too overdressed in comparison.

I selected a soft green sundress that would look cute and professional while at the same time looking casual to fit the setting. I'd pair it with some small silver earrings, nothing too fancy.

I nodded to myself, happy with my choices. All I had to do was wait for Piper to get out of the bathroom, and then I could head in there, get changed, and get all ready for my day.

Suddenly, though, I was hit by a bout of nausea. I swallowed hard, waiting for it to pass, closing my eyes to ward it off. Instead, the feeling intensified.

I rushed to the bathroom door, hesitating only a moment before bursting in so that I could throw up in the toilet. I hung there for a moment, feeling embarrassed. Here

I was, trying to make a good impression on everyone, and yet I'd had to interrupt Piper's shower so that I could puke. Yuck.

"Sorry," I mumbled.

"Are you okay?" Piper asked, poking her head out from around the shower curtain. "Had a little too much to drink last night?"

I shook my head. "No I barely drank at all last night. It must be some weird stomach bug," I told her. "I've been having it on and off all week."

Piper blinked at me, her mouth forming a little o. She shut off the water and reached for her towel, pulling it around herself before pushing the shower curtain open. I averted my gaze even though she was fully covered. "Don't you think that sounds like maybe..." She trailed off for a moment, then tried again. "When was the last time you had your period?"

I stared at her blankly, then started mentally doing the calculation. It was more difficult than it should have been for me to remember. Had I had one in the last month? I honestly didn't know.

"I don't know, things have been stressful since moving here," I said. "I don't remember if I've had one or not."

Piper gave me a skeptical look. "When you were with Jayson, did you use protection?" she asked gently.

"I mean, I'm on the pill," I told her.

She nodded slowly. "Well that's good, but it's not 100% effective. Did he use a condom?"

Oh fuck, oh fuck, oh fuck. The times that we had been together had been explosive and unexpected, so there had been no time for him to put on a condom. How could I have been so stupid?

I shook my head. "I'm sure it's just the stress and every-thing of the move and a new job. I'm sure that's all it is."

Piper looked skeptical but nodded her head. "Okay, maybe that's it. But when we get home, you should get checked out just in case. "Yeah," I said faintly. *Get checked out.* I hated to say it, but the idea of seeing a doctor, confirming whether or not I was pregnant, was terrifying. I was supposed to be focusing on my career. I could only imagine how much an unexpected pregnancy would derail things.

And what about Jayson? He wouldn't want anything to do with me if he found out that I was pregnant. He was in a band, one that was just about to take off. They were in the studio even now, working on an album. He wouldn't want to be tied down by a girl, and he definitely wouldn't want to be tied down by a baby. He wasn't in the "family" portion of his life. He might never be.

Could I handle having a baby all on my own so far away from my family? I didn't know if I could. I had only been in LA a couple of months. I still barely knew anyone there. There would be no one to help me out. All the friends I had started to make, I was sure to lose. Piper and the rest of them were at different places in their lives. They didn't have kids; they weren't even thinking about kids yet, not in the near future anyway.

I tried not to panic. The last thing I wanted was to spend the rest of the retreat panicking in the bathroom. I didn't want Piper to feel like she had to take care of me. Hell, I didn't want her to know that anything was wrong in the first place. I wasn't pregnant. I *wasn't.*

I forced a smile on my face and flushed the toilet. "Why don't I get out of here so you can finish?" I suggested. "Then we'll head over to breakfast and get on with our meetings. I need you to help me figure out who's who again before I talk to them all one-on-one later."

"Sure thing," Piper said. I could see the open concern still on her face, and I didn't want to admit how that rattled me.

Nor did I want to admit how badly I bombed my one-on-one with the bosses a little while later. I was flustered, and I was having a hard time focusing. I felt too warm and cold in waves, and even though I didn't feel nauseous anymore, I didn't feel right, either. I was still tired, even though I had gone to bed early the night before.

I couldn't stop thinking about the possibility that I was pregnant. I knew I wasn't going to be able to devote my full attention to anything else until I knew the truth.

I felt demoralized and scared as I walked out of there. Piper, of course, was waiting to hear how things had gone. She could probably tell how terrible it was from the look on my face, and she wisely didn't ask.

"I need to sneak out of here early," I told her miserably, shaking my head. I thought of how much fun I had been having prior to getting sick that morning. If only I could go back to that.

I wanted to stick it out to the end of the day. We were due for some more camp shenanigans that afternoon before heading out. What was I rushing back to, anyway? Reality and finding out that I might actually be pregnant. And then what, confronting Jayson? Nine months of misery, or whatever remained of those nine months? Sleepless nights, probably having to move back home and forget about my dreams for good?

Couldn't I just have one more day of fun before I needed to deal with all of that? Now that the seeds of doubt had been planted in my brain, though, they were impossible to forget.

Piper held out her keys to me. "I'll get a ride home with someone," she said. "I'll even bring your things if you need."

I frowned, chewing at my lower lip. "I already screwed up with the bosses," I said. "I don't want them to think I'm the kind of person who runs away from their responsibilities."

Piper shrugged. "I'll tell them you had a family emergency," she said. "If you want, I'll tell them you found out about it right before you went in there and that's why you were so rattled. It's technically true, isn't it?"

I sighed. "I guess so," I said. I didn't resist as she pulled me into a hug. God, at least I had a friend like her, even if it might not last once I had the kid. If only we'd had a little more time to cement our friendship before we got to that point.

"Get out of here," Piper said.

"Thanks," I said, already thinking ahead to what I needed to do to get out of there. I had driven to the office and then carpooled up here with Piper and some of the other girls. "I'll leave your car at work and your keys in the top drawer of your desk. I can take my own car home from there."

She shook her head. "Don't worry about it. Just let me know how it goes. If you're not, you know, I'll bring over a bottle of wine. And if you are, then your favorite ice cream. I promise."

I laughed in spite of myself. "Thanks," I repeated. "I'll talk to you soon."

My hands were shaking as I climbed into her car. It took me two tries to get the key into the ignition, and I wondered if it was even safe for me to drive at the moment. I couldn't head back out there into the camp, though. I had to get out of here. I had to *know*.

I stopped at the first drugstore I saw on the way back, grabbing a pregnancy test and paying for it without looking the cashier in the eye. I headed into the drugstore bathroom and took the test right then and there, not able to wait any longer. The two minutes it took for the results to show on the stick seemed like an eternity.

I stared down at the thing for a long moment, my heart stopping and the air rushing out of me.

Positive.

I really was pregnant. Piper had been right. My stomach churned with worry, and I sank down to a seat on the lid of the toilet.

Pregnant. Fuck. What the hell was I going to do now?

JAYSON

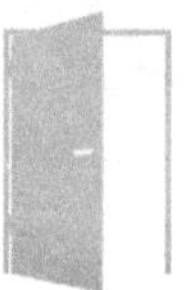

It had been far too long since I'd seen Leah. I'd gotten used to being near her so frequently, and those two weeks left me missing her. The gap her absence left in my day had me looking forward to when she would be back from wherever she'd gone. It was a strange realization. I wasn't used to having that sort of attachment to anyone. The guys in my band were one thing, but there weren't times during the day when I thought about them or wondered what they were doing when I wasn't with them.

Not like with Leah. I thought about her all day when she was gone. Just going about my life throwing laundry in to wash or warming up leftover pizza to eat standing over the sink, I'd find myself thinking about her. My mind wandered to our time together, to the sound of her laugh and the smell of her skin. A few times I heard something and wanted to tell her about it. I almost couldn't believe it had been two damn weeks. I needed to see her and could hardly wait for her to get back.

A jolt of excitement went through me when I pulled into the driveway and saw her car sitting there. Part of me thought I should give her the chance to settle back in, but the much bigger, much more determined part of me wasn't having any of it. She was right there, so close, and I wasn't going to miss an opportunity to see her before we both got busy again and another week or two went by. I freshened up and walked up to her door. There was a pause after my knock, but she finally opened it. When she did, I could tell right away something was bothering her.

"Welcome home," I said, and she tried to give a convincing smile. "What's wrong?"

Leah shook her head, working harder at masking what she was feeling behind the faked smile. There was definitely something wrong. Worry slithered up through me.

"Nothing," she said. "Just recovering from the weekend, that's all."

I narrowed my eyes at her slightly, examining her face and waiting for her to continue. When she didn't, I took a step closer to her. Taking both her hands in mine, I held them between us.

"Are you sure?" I asked.

She nodded. "Yep."

I wasn't convinced. She was looking at me, but there was something missing in her eyes. It was like she was looking somewhere else. Something was getting to her, digging at her, but I knew enough to know she wasn't going to tell me any more. Whatever it was, she needed time to think through it on her own before she told me about it. All I could do was be there for her.

"I can't believe it's been two weeks since we've seen each other," I said, hoping to start a conversation.

She nodded and looked away again. "Yeah, it's been

pretty crazy. Work's been busy and I had a company retreat this weekend. How have you been?"

"I've been busy too. The band's been practicing and we're actually recording too. Things are better."

She gave me a ghost of a smile. "That's good to hear. Listen, I'm really tired –" she started.

I cut her off. I wasn't willing to let her push me away just yet.

"Have you eaten dinner yet?" I asked.

Leah shook her head. "Not yet. I hadn't even thought about it."

"Well, now you don't have to. I'm going to take you out."

She hesitated. "I don't know. It was kind of a long week-end, and I'm not really feeling up to getting dressed up and going out."

"You don't need to. You're perfect just the way you are. Come on. You have to eat, and there's this awesome little place I've been wanting to show you. It's one of my favorites," I told her.

She looked down at her jeans and T-shirt.

"Honestly, you're gorgeous. Let's go."

She finally nodded and ducked inside to put on shoes before following me out to my car. We drove to the beach, and I led her to a rickety old restaurant perched near the water. It used to be a hot spot among the tourists, but now it was a hidden gem treasured by locals not looking for anything fancy.

"I've never been here," Leah told me as I pulled a chair out for her.

"It's one of my favorite places. The food here is incredi-ble. And it's not pretentious like some of the other places around," I told her.

Amazing seafood and inexpensive prices, not to

mention being off the beaten path so I was unlikely to run into anyone, made it the perfect place to have a relaxing dinner just with Leah. We settled in and ordered. As the waitress came by with hot crusty bread and a plate of butter, I started telling her about my music. She nibbled on a chunk of bread and listened intently as I told her how well the studio sessions were going.

"That's good to hear," she said, her voice sounding distant.

"Yeah. We're really meshing. Everything is clicking, and I'm happier with the music we're making than I have been in a long time. The album is going to be amazing. I can't wait to hear the final product," I said. Leah nodded, staring down at the bread in her hand. She was still preoccupied, and I hoped to find out what was going on with her, so I made a pivot in the conversation. "How about you?"

Her eyes snapped up to me. "Me?"

The waitress came with our food, and I paused until she walked away.

"Yeah. How was your retreat?" I asked.

Maybe something happened there that was still bothering her. I knew how much her work meant to her, so if it didn't go well, that could explain why she seemed distracted. Leah grimaced.

"Actually, it didn't go as well as I hoped," she admitted. "I'm really disappointed."

"I'm sorry to hear that. But I'm sure you'll be able to turn things around. You're too smart and driven not to. It will end up even better than you thought," I told her.

Leah managed a small, genuine smile and picked up her fork. "Thanks."

We ate and chatted, falling to a rhythm of easy conversation and comfortable silence. She seemed to relax and loosen up some as the evening went on, and by the time we finished eating, I knew I didn't want it to be done yet.

"How about a walk on the beach?" I asked as we left the restaurant. "It's a really pretty evening."

She nodded. "That would be nice."

I led her a distance away from the restaurant and down onto a stretch of sand most people didn't realize was publicly accessible. It was quiet and empty, just like I expected it to be. The sun was setting, making the surface of the water glow and shimmer with shades of pink and orange. It cast a sultry, romantic light across the beach, and I held Leah's hand as we strolled slowly along the sand. She reached down and took off her shoes so she could bury her toes in the sand dampened by the waves.

Wanting to savor the last seconds of the sunset, I paused and pulled Leah into my arms. Holding her with her back against my chest, I wrapped my arms around her waist and rested my chin gently on the top of her head. Letting out a sigh, I enjoyed the feeling of her against me as we watched the sun slip beneath the horizon. It spread vibrant light across the sky and melted down into the waves. Leah released her own long breath and relaxed back against me, one hand rested over mine.

"I want you to know you are a big reason this album is going to be such a success," I said softly.

She shifted, tilting her head slightly as if to look up at me but not taking her eyes away from the last lingering bit of the sunset.

"What do you mean?" she asked. "I haven't done anything."

"Yes, you have. Just being in my life has made all the difference. Meeting and getting to know you has been so inspiring. My lyrics has never been stronger. I'm creating like I haven't been able to in as long as I can remember. Maybe like I never have before. It's all thanks to you," I told her.

Releasing my arms from around her, I turned her slightly and tucked a finger under her chin to lift her face. I lowered a kiss to her lips, meaning for it to be just a soft, tender touch. As soon as our mouths met, I was overwhelmed by the intensity of the feelings and the moment building around us. I kissed her harder, the rush between us escalating quickly until I knew I couldn't resist her. I needed her and wasn't going to be able to make it off the beach, much less all the way back to my apartment.

Her shoes dropped from her hand, and she looped her arms around my neck, opening her mouth to deepen the kiss. Our tongues tangled, and I forced myself to break the kiss and step back from her. Looking around, I spied an empty cove not far away. As night descended around us, I pulled Leah across the beach and into the shadow of the cove. As soon as we were in the private space, I swept her into my arms again and ducked my head down for another kiss. When our mouths parted, I brought my lips to the side of her neck.

Leah moaned softly as I ran my tongue along the soft flesh, savoring the sweetness of her skin until I reached her lips. We kissed languidly and lay back against the sand, our bodies melding into one another. The heat radiating off of us was stifling and only served to add another desperate reason to disrobe. As her fingers worked the buttons of my shirt, I pulled at the hem of her skirt, bunching it above her hips, and the cool air on my chest set a chill down my spine. I grabbed a handful of her ass and pulled her into me, and she broke our kiss to look up with eyes full of excitement and desire. One hand slid down my chest to my crotch and grasped my hardened cock over my jeans. I moaned at her touch.

Suddenly, Leah stood, crossing her arms in front of her and pulling at her blouse. Up and over her head it went, and the dying sunlight glistened on the beads of sweat between her breasts. I licked my lips in anticipation and undid my belt. Undoing the buttons on the side of her sundress, she straddled me and sat down, rubbing her hot, wet core against me without removing her panties. I grasped her by the hips and guided her in long, slow motions over me, and one of her arms reached behind her. She was searching for my zipper, and I pulled her closer so she sat on my chest while she found it. A whiff of her arousal mixed with the salty sea air piqued my erection even more, and I felt like I was going to burst through my pants by the time she relieved the stress of the zipper. I continued to pull her closer to my mouth as her hand searched for the open flap in my boxers.

I had her close enough now, and she lifted herself on her knees above me. My cock sprang out of my boxers and into the cool air as I clenched her panties with my teeth and pushed them aside. As her fingers wrapped around my base and stroked up for the first time, I plunged my tongue inside of her, and she let out a cry of pleasure. With a long, patient lick, I worked my way to her pearl, and her grip on my cock got tighter.

22

LEAH

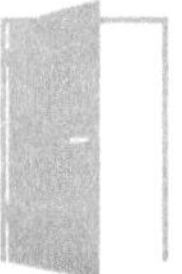

I leaned my head back and let the sound come out of me with abandon. We were out in the open, more or less, and at any moment someone could come by and see us. Yet, it was secluded enough that it felt like our own little world, and the heightened sense of urgency to not get caught only made it hotter. I had barely gotten his cock out of his boxers, and already I was trembling, dancing on the edge of a powerful orgasm. I breathed out slowly, sound still tumbling out uncontrolled as his tongue slid through my folds and found my clit.

Jayson's thick, long cock twitched, and I grasped it, stroking it passionately as I leaned back, giving him better access to me. His tongue worked its way through me, lapping me up and pleasuring me in ways I had never felt before. My legs trembled and one hand reached out to fill with his hair as a climactic wave rushed over my body. I bucked and leaned forward, my hands digging into the sand while the thunderous climax took complete control of my body. I didn't care how exposed I was to any passersby. All that mattered in that moment was letting him fill me, to feel him inside of me and to continue this feeling of intense pleasure.

As I came down from the climax, Jayson shifted below me, wiggling until he was out from underneath me. I sensed him position himself behind me as I stayed on my hands and knees. Fingers, searching and finding what they desired, traced my body as the head of his cock lay against my mound, sliding backward to find my opening. At first, he placed himself there, not moving, but waiting. The anticipation of him filling me was tantalizing and maddening. I wanted him inside me, I wanted to feel him stretch me, but he stayed there, strong, confident hands holding my hips in place.

I looked back and our eyes met, a smirk crossing his face. Then he plunged into me, deeply, roughly. My mouth opened, but no sound came out. I was hovering at the line of pain and pleasure, and I leaned down, pushing my hips into him. He stretched me, pushing himself deeper still until he filled me completely. Holding it there, his hands slid up my waist and up to my bra, pulling at the clasp in the front and releasing my heavy breasts from its grip. As they dropped down, the cool air brushed over them, and my nipples hardened even more than they were. His large, warm hands quickly covered them, kneading into me and pulling me into him even more.

He was hunched over me, one arm crossing over one breast, his hand holding the other. His other hand filled with a handful of my hair and pulled, gentle enough not to hurt me, but hard enough to establish his dominance. I was his, openly and completely, and his body was dominating mine. His body began to rock back and forth into me, slamming his cock deeply inside as he held me in place with his arms. Soft, wet lips kissed my neck, and his tongue swept away sweat before his teeth clenched over my shoulder. I cried out in surprise but reached up to wrap one arm around his neck. I didn't want him to stop.

Releasing me from his mouth, Jayson straightened behind me, his hands sliding to my hips and guiding me in his long thrusts. With each plunge, an involuntary sound broke free and mingled with the sound of the soft waves. He gained speed, letting adrenaline and desire take over, and I relished his power. I arched back so I could take him as deeply as possible, and the thrusts became rhythmic and measured. My fingers dug into the sand as I closed my eyes, letting the moment stretch on timelessly. Naked and exposed on the beach, I felt more vulnerable and yet thrilled than I ever had, and I wanted to live in it, to hold on to the feeling of reckless abandon for as long as possible.

Suddenly, Jayson slid out of me, and I turned back to look at him. He was standing and held one hand out to me to stand with him. Curious, I took it and wondered what he was thinking. We walked a few steps to one side of the cove, overlooking a few sand dunes and a crooked edge of the beach. A rock that stood almost to hip height was there, its smooth top flattened and shaded during the day by large palm trees above it. As we reached the rock, he turned me toward him and crushed his mouth into mine for a deep kiss. As our tongues searched one another, he lifted me up by my ass and planted me on the smooth stone. I gasped at the coldness of it despite the heat of the beach and lay back.

Positioning himself in front of me, Jayson pulled me

until my hips were at the edge of the rock, and my legs rested on his shoulders. I stared up at the dying sunlight and the stars making their first appearances in a clear, dim blue sky as he placed his cock at my entrance. I arched up as he thrust himself inside of me again, and a moan bubbled up from within me at the daring way we were now perched, out in the open and only shaded by a few trees and the slowly disappearing light of the day. I tried to focus on his muscular chest as the sweat glistened off it and rolled in streams down the ridges and valleys of his abs. He leaned over me, bending my legs back toward my chest and thrusting in fluid and strong motions.

I could feel him increasing his speed, edging closer to his own climax, but selfishly I wanted it to last longer. I wanted to taste him, to pleasure him the way he pleasured me, before he was completely spent. I curled my legs up and turned away from him, and for a moment he stopped. I beckoned him to switch places, and he did happily. Rather than lay him down and mount him, I knelt into the sand in front of him. His throbbing cock hovered just in front of my lips, and I looked up into his eyes. I kept the eye contact as I ran my tongue along the underside of him, swirling it at the head and then taking it into my mouth. It pulsed against my tongue as I tightened my mouth around him and pushed down toward the base. I took as much of him as I could into my mouth, until I could feel the tip brush against the back of my throat, and then slid him back out again. He moaned loudly above me, and I smiled at the sound.

Clasping one hand around the base, I let the other slide up to cup his balls, gently kneading them as I bobbed on his cock, stroking him into my mouth and tasting the mixture of our sweat and sex. His hand slipped around my head and filled with my hair, and I let him guide me in the motion. For a moment I was slow and passionate, but I quickly gained speed. I sucked on him, twirling my tongue around and twisting as I reached the tip, and his legs clenched as he tried to maintain control. I reveled in the thought that he was trying to keep from exploding right then, and took him deeper into my mouth, letting him slide as far down my throat as I could stand.

His moans turned to a growl, and I knew he was close. I stood up quickly and wrapped one leg around him. He lifted me, holding me by my ass and pushing me against the palm tree. I clenched around him, taking him deeply inside of me as our mouths searched for each other and met in a hard kiss. He bounced me on his cock, my back braced against the tree, and I cried out against his mouth as a dizzying orgasm crashed around me. My legs shook and I wrapped my arms around his neck, clenching my entire body around him. Jayson exploded into me, roaring as he climaxed and emptied himself into me. He held me there for some time as my body milked him, and I kissed the sweat off his neck and chest.

Finally, his body spent, he gently lowered me back to the sand, curling beside me, and our noses touched as we stared into each other's eyes. We lay there, naked and free, without a care between us as the stars took over the velvet sky.

I had never felt so close to Jayson as when I was lying there in his arms, still riding the last waves of pleasure. I had probably never felt so close to anyone. In those moments it felt like we had transcended just being two people enjoying each other and instead melded into something much more. It was an incredible feeling, something I wanted to cherish and hold on to for as long as possible. That brought a thought to my mind and to my heart.

Maybe all these worries were for nothing. Maybe my doubts were foolish. After all, I hadn't even really given myself a chance to think all the way through this. As soon as I found out I was pregnant, all I let myself do was worry and go immediately to the worst-case scenario. My mind jumped straight to not being able to trust anyone and how devastating this could be rather than thinking even for a second that things might work out.

This could be my moment. This could be the time when I finally allow myself to take a chance and reach out to someone. As I lay there with my head on Jayson's chest, listening to his heartbeat and breathing in the smell of him, I thought about what could be. Maybe I should take a chance and open my heart to him. If there was ever a time in my life when it would be right to open up and show my true self, this would be it. I drew in a breath and tried to come up with the right words. This wasn't something I'd ever done and wasn't sure exactly how to tell him. I wanted to tell him how I was feeling and about the baby. I didn't know how he was going to react, but the way he cradled me in his arms and kissed the side of my head put me at ease.

The words were just starting to form in my mind, and I opened my mouth to speak, but right at that moment I heard the sound of revving engines. Bright round lights cut through the darkness, and I gasped as I saw two sets of beams coming right in our direction. Jayson shot out from under me and jumped to his feet, reaching down to grab onto my hands. He pulled me up frantically and reached down for his pants.

"What's going on?" I asked.

He hopped on one foot as he got into his pants as fast as

he could, and I followed suit, wriggling back into my pants and reaching for my bra.

"It's the beach patrol," he told me. "Put your dress on. We've got to get out of here before they catch us."

I dropped my dress over my head and scooped up my bra and panties just as he grabbed hold of my wrist and started pulling me out of the cove. He laughed as he took off running, pulling me behind him. It was all happening so fast, but his laughter was infectious. I couldn't help but laugh too as I struggled to keep up with him. We got out onto the beach and paused just long enough to snatch my shoes up from the sand where I'd dropped them when he first kissed me. The lights were following us across the beach, and I heard someone shout in the distance, so we ran faster.

We got back to the parking lot, and Jayson flung himself forward across the hood of his car. I leaned back against the door, laughing as we struggled to catch our breath.

"I think we lost them," I said.

"Good thing. We wouldn't want to end up with our picture by the door at the restaurant," Jayson told me.

"What?" I gasped.

He laughed harder. "You didn't see them? The beach patrol goes up and down the beach every night, and if they catch people getting cozy, they take pictures of them. Clothed pictures," he clarified. "They bring them to the restaurant, and they get posted."

"That's awful!" I said but couldn't help but laugh more. "Can you imagine going in to have dinner and seeing yourself up on the wall?"

Jayson shrugged and walked up to me, sliding his hands around my waist again. "It would be worth it."

A slow smile slid onto his face, and he leaned down for

another soft kiss. When it ended, I pulled back and looked up at him. The words were right there on the tip of my tongue, but something was still holding me back. The moment didn't feel right anymore. I decided to wait, to enjoy our burgeoning romance a little more before finding the perfect time to tell him about the pregnancy.

23

JAYSON

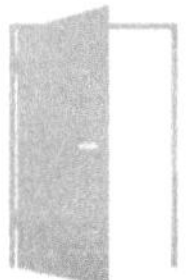

The band was still riding high on the adrenaline from the wave of success we were experiencing, and it made our practice even more thrilling and intense. We were all still pumped about the reception of the album and the buzz it was already creating. Rather than letting it lull us into complacency, though, it was revving us up and making us even more determined. We were reaching a peak like we hadn't in a long time, and all of us were thrilled to be a part of it.

Only a week after we finished the album, it was already making waves among important people in the music industry. It wasn't hitting the radio stations yet, and it would be a while before it got onto shelves, but that would come. For now, we had to concentrate on making sure the right people heard it. These were the people who would give us more time in studios and hook us up with the artists, producers, and others who could catapult us to the next level. Getting that was a more important first step than reaching out to listeners. The fans would come, but only if there was a way for them to hear us. That meant needing exposure, and that meant impressing the right people.

Fortunately, that's exactly what our brand-new agent was doing for us. It was still hard to believe we even had an agent. Of course, this type of success was what we'd always wanted. We hadn't just thrown together a band because we thought it would be fun to jam together, or even for the attention from local fans. Though the dedicated groupies we picked up rather quickly were a nice perk while we built up. All of us came together over a love of music and a true drive to really make something out of ourselves. We looked ahead to the days when we would have huge audiences and be able to walk into any music store and see our album. Now it seemed like it was actually happening. We had a real agent, and he was getting copies of our album into the hands of some of the most powerful people in the industry.

I couldn't wait to see what would happen next, and it turned out, I didn't have to. When we wrapped up our practice, Luke looked at us with a grin.

"Hold on, guys. I need to talk to you," he said.

"What's up?" Mark asked.

Luke held out his arms dramatically, directing us to sit down on the gray-blue couch that occupied the edge of our practice space. We rolled our eyes but went along with it. Luke looked like he was going to bounce out of his skin as Carter, Mark, and I dropped down on the couch and stared at him. Finally, he grinned.

"I have an announcement to make. As manager, you know I've been working closely with Greg to get our album out there in front of people," he said.

"And by that you mean he's been doing all the work and you've been telling us about it?" Mark teased.

Luke gave him a look but continued.

"We've been making progress, but this morning I got word that something big is happening. Who here has heard of a little band called The Monsters?"

It was purely for dramatic effect. The Monsters had gotten pretty successful recently and were about to go on a major tour.

"Yes," I said to push Luke forward. I really wasn't feeling like sitting around the practice space for the rest of the day waiting for him to continue regaling us.

"Well, it just so happens they were looking for a band to open for them while they're on the road. Greg got them a copy of our album, and they called to offer us the spot," Luke concluded.

The three of us sat silently for a beat, not really believing him. When he didn't say he was joking, we exchanged glances and I looked back at him.

"Are you serious?" I asked.

"Absolutely," Luke answered. "They're starting their North American tour soon, and they want us to come along. It's a huge opportunity. At least a year of shows, a per diem, the whole thing. We could seriously catch on while we're going and end up with another tour."

Excitement bubbled up and soon we were all talking over each other, giving high fives, and making plans. I couldn't believe this was finally happening. It was everything we wanted.

The reality didn't sink in until after I left the practice space and headed home. As I drove toward the apartments, I thought of Leah. I couldn't wait to tell her about the tour and how excited I was to get on the road and start really touring. She was going to be so proud and excited for us. As soon as that thought went through my mind, it hit me. This wasn't just about me going on tour with the band and what that could mean for the future of my career.

It also forced me to think about the future of the rest of my life, including my relationship with Leah. Things had been going well since that day at the beach and I was truly happy. But accepting the tour offer meant we'd be on the road for a year. There would be shows several days a week, and when we weren't performing, we'd be traveling or trying to find time to grab a little bit of sleep to fuel us through the next show. It wouldn't give us any time to come back home or take days off. Things were just getting serious with Leah. If I left for a year, who knew what would happen? Leaving for so long at this point in our relationship could mean losing everything we'd built up between us.

There was no way I could ask her to come with us. Some guys brought their girls along with them on tours, but they were the ones who had lives they could easily leave behind or jobs they could take with them. It wasn't like that with Leah. She was very focused on getting promoted at her dream job and achieving everything she set out for herself. It was just like me working hard to get further in my music career. It wouldn't be fair to ask her to come along and leave all that behind. It would be like her asking me to stop playing music.

But would there be any point in even trying to keep things going if I did go on the tour? Could we really be apart for that long and still have a relationship left alive when I finally came back home at the end of the tour? A year was a long time to be apart. It wasn't just a quick trip or a show or two. This was months and months away from each other. It was very likely there would be times when we weren't even able to talk on the phone for a few days at a time because of our conflicting schedules. I worried there would be no way to keep up our connection if we were living separate lives like that.

But it wasn't just about keeping up with a relationship or having a warm body to come home to when the long stretch of the tour was over. On the other end of the spectrum, I wasn't worried about not wanting to think about her, or the inconvenience of a long-distance relationship when I was on the road with fans throwing themselves at me. There would be women at the shows. Groupies like Trixie, new fans, devotees of The Monsters who weren't able to get their attention so they were willing to settle for anyone who could play music. It would be easy to bed a different woman every night if I wanted to. But I wasn't going to want to. Thinking about Leah back home wasn't going to hold me back or keep me from doing what I wanted to do, because I wasn't going to want to be with anyone but her.

I was in love with her. That wasn't even a question. I knew it with every fiber of my being. I wanted to be with her and really see where this relationship could take us. The thought of leaving her behind was painful and left me questioning everything. I didn't want to leave her, but at the same time, I couldn't pass up this opportunity. This was huge. Being able to open for The Monsters created a whole new world of potential for us. It put us in front of massive audiences that may never have heard of us in any other way. It gave us the chance to make an impression, reach out to new people, and network. This was a stepping stone to the type of success we wanted. I couldn't just walk away from that.

I didn't know what to do or how to handle the decision. By the time I got back to the apartment, the only thing I had decided was I couldn't tell Leah yet. As much as I wanted to share my excitement with her and tell her all about this new opportunity, I didn't want it to turn into the difficult, uncomfortable conversation I knew it would if I went into it without any idea of what we were going to do. She would ask questions I couldn't answer and bring up issues I didn't want to face.

Until I figured those things out, I wasn't going to bring it up. I would wait until I figured out a workable solution and continue to see how things were going for us. There was still a little bit of time before the tour started. It wasn't much, but it was enough to let me think and come to some decisions. Maybe it would work out better than I thought. Just because she couldn't get on the bus and come along on the tour with me didn't necessarily mean we had to be completely apart for the entire year.

Leah didn't work all day every day. She had breaks, vacations, weekends. There were times when she would be able to slip away. Some of our travel days would bring us far distances between shows, but it wasn't always that way. There were times when we would play a cluster of several shows right around in the same area. That would make it easy for her to take a few vacation days or plan a long weekend and come be with me. It wouldn't be the same as being able to see each other every day, but it would at least give us something to keep the relationship alive.

Even with that, I knew it wouldn't be easy. Long-distance relationships never were. I knew more than a few guys who tried to keep things up with women in different cities. Most of the conversations we had about their girls were about how hard it was to not be near them and how much they missed them. Some fell victim to the women who swarmed the audiences and crowded around the doors at the end of the shows. They had feelings for their girls back home, but sometimes that just wasn't enough to temper the craving for a warm body and some affection. Afterward they felt guilty and it hurt their relationship, their music, everything.

I wasn't going to let that happen. Whatever it took, I was going to protect both my career and my relationship with Leah. I was going to make it work. The first thing I needed to do was find out the tour schedule. That would give me an idea of where we would be and when so I could figure out opportunities to connect. When I had a full plan laid out and could show her all the times we would be able to see each other, then I would tell her about the tour.

LEAH

There was so much of a rush standing there in the audience, waiting for the show to start. It was unlike anything I'd experienced before I met Jayson. It wasn't just the music. That was enough to get my blood pumping, but there was so much more to it than that. It was him. It was knowing he was there and created the throbbing sounds. He woke up the audience and sent them into a frenzy. Somehow watching that happen and knowing I was the one he was thinking about, that of all the girls in the audience screaming for him, I was the only one he was paying atten-tion to, sent a thrill through me.

All around me, fans screamed and jumped up and down, trying to get the band's attention. They weren't even playing yet. The music around us was just a recording, warming us up for the live versions of the songs that would soon be playing. But the groupies didn't care. Anything having to do with these men got them going. The other guys looked out over the crowd and winked or waved, not necessarily directing it at any specific girl. That was the point. They could cast a wide net and any of them who thought that little acknowledgement was thrown their way would come to them at the end of the show and they would have their pick.

Not Jayson. He focused on getting his drums adjusted and making sure he was ready to play. Then he looked up and our eyes met. A smile stretched across his face when I waved at him. He waved back and winked. I knew that wink was just for me.

"You've got it bad," Piper said from beside me.

I looked over at her, then back at Jayson. He was back to concentrating on his drums, and I let out a breath, nodding.

"Yes, I do," I admitted.

We watched for another few seconds before Piper leaned slightly toward me.

"Have you told him yet?" she asked.

Even though the people around us were loud and not paying any attention to us, she lowered her voice so no one would overhear. I appreciated the discretion. Of all things I'd tried to keep to myself throughout my life, this was one I wanted to protect above all others.

"No," I said, shaking my head. "But I'm going to do it soon."

"Leah..." she started, and I pushed ahead, not wanting to hear her admonitions.

"I'm going to, Piper. It's just not the right time, yet. Right now, I'm just enjoying being close to him. Nothing is going to be the same once I tell him. I just want to enjoy some time with him before everything changes," I told her.

It made sense to me, and I wanted it to make sense to her. I needed that time. Our relationship was so good, and I had fallen so hard for Jayson. He made me happy like no one ever had and watching him climb through his career was amazing. It was fulfilling, and I couldn't wait to see how much more he could accomplish. Telling him about the pregnancy would completely change everything. I still didn't know how that change would unfold or what it would mean, but I knew it would change. I wanted to build a stronger foundation first.

"It won't be much longer before you don't really have the option to tell him," Piper pointed out. "You don't want to get to that point. Tell him before he figures it out for himself."

"I'm going to. I'm going to tell him soon."

At that moment, I was saved from the awkward conversation by Luke jumping down off the stage and coming toward us. He was the only one of the four other than Jayson who might not have been throwing winks and blowing kisses to anyone who would look at him. His might have been directed at one specific person, and I knew just who that was.

There was a distinct swagger to his walk as he made his way up to Piper and grinned at her.

"Hey, Piper," he said. "You look beautiful tonight."

Piper looked down at the black jeans and plain white T-shirt she was wearing. I knew for a fact it was what she'd worn to work that day with the only change being taking off a cardigan. Working late meant she didn't have a chance to put on anything else, and the ride over to the show only gave her enough time to take off the sweater and throw on some of the makeup I kept in my glove compartment for such emergencies. But it was a sweet sentiment.

"Thank you, Luke," she said. "Are you excited for the show?"

"More excited now that I know you're here," he said.

They were slipping into flirting, and I couldn't help but smile. Taking a step back, I gave them more space and watched. The bassist wasn't a bad fit for my friend. He would be good to her, and it was obvious how much he liked her. I had to feel bad for him, though. Piper was basically torturing him. She went to the shows and danced, flirting with him from the audience and chatting with him after he played. But she never went home with him. That was going to take some time.

The thing was, I knew Piper was into Luke. She might not have ever come right out and said it, but I could see it when she looked at him and heard the way she talked about him. She just wasn't easy. She definitely wasn't one of the groupies or even just a casual fan who wanted a thrill. Piper thought of herself much more highly than that. She liked it when guys put in an effort and tended to carry it along for a while to see if they would be willing to keep it going. So far, Luke was doing a pretty good job. He made sure Piper knew he was thinking about her and gave her special attention. She hadn't caught him with anyone else. I was feeling fairly confident they would hook up soon.

"You know, I'm not going to play as well on the road if you're not there. You're just going to have to come on tour with us," Luke said.

At first, it sounded like he was teasing, but then I realized he was serious. My eyes widened.

"Wait, what?" I asked.

Luke looked over at me like he had forgotten I was even there. His eyes narrowed slightly.

"The tour," he said. "Didn't Jayson tell you?"

"Didn't Jayson tell her what?" Piper asked, sounding slightly impatient and wanting to get the attention back on her.

It worked and Luke turned back to her with a wide smile.

"The Monsters have hired us to open for them on their national tour," he told her.

Piper's face lit up, and she gasped. "That's incredible! Congratulations! I'm so excited for you. That means big things for you, right?"

Luke nodded. "Yeah, it does. The Monsters are really moving up, and we can ride their popularity right to the big times."

Piper laughed and moved slightly closer to him, her flirting reaching epic new levels now.

"Does that mean I can get comped tickets since I know the band?" she asked.

She was clearly excited, and I had a feeling this revelation was going to put them on the fast track to something much more than flirting. But I was devastated. My mind was reeling, and I could barely even hear the conversation going on between them. Jayson hadn't even mentioned the tour to me. This was huge, a major step in his career and the potential for the band, but he hadn't said anything to me about it. Did that mean he didn't even consider me worth knowing about it? Maybe he didn't think it would matter.

But it was more than that. It wasn't just about him not telling me about the tour or what that might mean about his feelings for me. There was no way he could be a father and also be on the road. These tours were long and intense. He would barely have enough time to himself to breathe and eat. He wouldn't be able to be an active part of our baby's life.

In that instant, all my plans changed. I wasn't waiting for the perfect moment to tell him about my pregnancy anymore. I had to keep quiet about it and not let him ever know. Jayson was a good guy. If I told him about the baby, he wouldn't want to leave me without his help. He would want to be there for the pregnancy and definitely after the baby was born. He might do something noble like insist on quitting the band so he didn't have to go on tour. That would kill his dreams.

Of course, that wasn't the worst that could happen. As much as I didn't want to think about him giving up something he'd worked so hard for, what was even worse was thinking about him leaving me altogether. He could break up with me and disappear. That was a rejection I didn't think I could handle.

I couldn't stop thinking about it for the rest of the show. Every time Jayson looked at me, I tried to smile and look like I was enjoying myself, but I was distracted. After the show, we met outside and he brought me home.

Rather than walking me to my door, he took my hand and guided me to his apartment. As soon as we were inside, he gathered me in his arms and ducked his head down for a kiss. He moved his mouth to the side of my neck and kissed along it until he reached my ear.

"I'm going to spend the next several hours making long, slow love to you," he whispered. He drew my earlobe into his mouth and bit down playfully. "I'm going to show you that every inch of your body belongs to me."

I could have stopped him there. I could have pulled away from him and told him I knew about the tour. Or not. I could have just pulled away and told him not that night and we would talk the next day. But I couldn't. He felt so good so close to me, and I didn't want to be away from him. That night possibly more than ever before, I needed him.

My mouth found his and we kissed deeply. There was no rush, no urgency behind it. I didn't want to waste even a second or hurry through any of the moments I had with him. This was to savor him, to enjoy every bit of him I could. I concentrated on the feeling of his hands on my body and the taste of his tongue sliding across mine. There was a faint hint of the drinks he'd had at the bar, and I knew I would always remember that taste. I wanted to memorize him, to etch into my memory every single detail I possibly could so that when the time came I was away from him and found myself missing him, I could call them to mind.

Because I knew that was it. This wasn't going to be something I could carry on or try to work out. Jayson didn't know it, but that night as I kissed him with everything in me and offered my body over to him, we were saying goodbye.

JAYSON

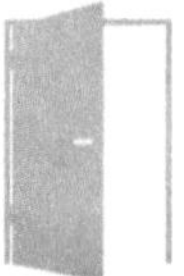

Leah kissed me, pressing her body against mine and opening her mouth so I could taste the softness of her tongue. She wrapped her arms around my neck, digging her fingers into my hair as if trying to hold me closer and anchor herself to me. I held her against me, feeling the warmth of her body and the lushness of her curves.

I had plans for the night. It stretched on long in front of us, and I wanted to fill every second of it with worshipping her. My body craved her; my heart ached for her. She was mine, and I wanted to show her that so she wouldn't have any way to question it. The journey we were on together was only getting better by the day, and I couldn't wait to see what was ahead of us. As I guided her back into my bedroom, undressing her as we went, I no longer had even the hint of worry or fear about the tour coming up. It didn't matter if we had to be away from each other between shows. It didn't matter if we were only able to see each other for a few hours or a couple of days each time when she was able to get away. We would be fine. We would work it out. This was real, and nothing was going to take us apart.

We got into my bedroom, and I broke the kiss so I could lower myself to my knees in front of her. I'd already gotten her shirt off on our way into the bedroom, and I leaned forward to kiss her stomach. My hands slid up her thighs and under her skirt, taking hold of her panties so I could guide them down her legs. Leah rested her hands on my shoulders to hold herself steady as she lifted her feet so I could remove the scrap of lace and toss it aside.

My mouth touched the inside of one ankle and made its way up along the inside of her leg until I found the tenderness just before her core. She shivered, but I didn't give her the satisfaction she desired. Instead, I moved my mouth over to the other leg and repeated the trail of kisses. Leah moaned and her hands left my shoulders to release the zipper on her skirt. I tugged it away and finally she was completely bare. She was mine, vulnerable and beautiful. I'd never felt like this about a woman, and I just wanted it to continue. I would happily drown in the happiness I found with her.

Guiding her legs apart, I brought my mouth between her thighs and drew my tongue through her center. She let out a shuddering breath and dropped down into my arms. I gathered her close as I sat back, settling her into my lap. As our lips played against each other and my hand slipped into her slick warmth, I used my other hand to finish undressing.

Soon I was inside her, buried deep so our bodies melded to one another. I used one hand to rock her hips while the other swirled over her clit. Leah's head fell back, and I quickly took my hand away. She looked at me with disappointment, and I smiled.

"Not yet. Slow. We have all night," I whispered to her.

A distant look crossed her eyes, and for a moment, she looked sad. Then she leaned forward and brushed her lips across mine. I swept the tip of my tongue across them and bent my legs to hold her closer, filling as much of the space around our bodies as I could.

I made love to her for hours, bringing her to the point of trembling and crying out in bliss over and over until I couldn't hold out anymore. I came hard, spilling out into her as she clung to me, kissing my neck and shoulders with something close to desperation. My mouth settled onto hers, and I gave myself over to another kiss. Our bodies and spirits became one, and in that moment, everything was perfect.

* * *

Morning came before I wanted it to that day. The bed was so comfortable, and I'd slept deeply, enjoying having Leah right there beside me. All I wanted to do was stay like that. Maybe I could convince her to play hooky from work for the day and hide under the covers with me. I was sure I could come up with a compelling cover story that would excuse her not being there. Some creativity and a little bit of stretching reality would definitely be worth spending the day ordering takeout and pretending nothing outside existed alongside Leah.

But it seemed I was too late coming up with that plan. When I rolled over to kiss her awake and try to convince her to forego work in favor of a day hiding out from the world with me, I found the other half of the bed empty. Getting up, I went over to the bathroom, but the door was open. The rest of the apartment was empty. It disappointed me but wasn't that much of a surprise. It was fairly late in the morning, and Leah had probably already left for work. She knew how much shows exhausted me and wanted to give me the chance to sleep it off some. It was nice, but I would have rather her wake me up to say goodbye.

I went about the rest of my day and figured Leah had to work late because by the time I had to leave for rehearsal, she still wasn't back. It wasn't the first time that had happened. Getting this promotion worked her hard, and she often stayed away well after normal work hours. I texted her a few times from practice, but she didn't respond. The next morning, I still hadn't heard from her, and when I left to run some errands, her car wasn't sitting in the driveway. I called her again, this time leaving a voicemail.

"Hey, Leah. It's me. I just haven't heard from you in a couple days and was thinking about you. Miss you. Don't work yourself too hard, okay? Let's have dinner tonight. We can go back to the seafood place. Or something else if you'd rather. Just come on by when you get home from work." I hesitated, leaving a pause. "Bye."

I almost filled that space with "I love you." It would fit in, feel right, but I didn't say it. As much as I felt it, that wasn't something Leah and I had said to each other, yet. I didn't want the first time for her to hear it to be when I was leaving her a voicemail wondering where she was.

That evening I waited for her to knock on the door. It got later and she didn't come, so I walked to her door and knocked on it. She didn't answer, and I checked the driveway. Her car still wasn't there. Another series of texts went unanswered, and I was starting to feel like a pathetic sap in some bad TV movie. Even that didn't stop me from wanting to find her. Worry was really starting to settle in, and I just wanted to make sure she was safe. I called again, but this time it went straight to voicemail. There wasn't even the nicety of a ring.

I tried not to think about it for the rest of the night. There had to be some sort of explanation. She was working more, or something had happened with a friend who needed her help. The ideas of what could have happened became more and more of a stretch throughout the night until I finally fell asleep. I slept late the next day and woke up to the sound of a car pulling up in front of the building. Looking out the window, I saw the landlord climb out of his car and reach into the back seat. He came out with a sign and planted it in the lawn.

I rushed out and caught him just before he drove away.

"For Rent?" I asked. "Why is there a 'For Rent' sign?"

He rolled down the window and peered out at me.

"What?" he asked.

I pointed at the sign. "What's this for?"

"The other unit is for rent again," he said.

"What do you mean it's for rent? Where's Leah?"

"I don't know. She didn't leave a forwarding address. Just paid the rent for next month and told me she was leaving. Hopefully I'll find someone to move in before that runs out."

Without another word, he rolled up the window, waved, and drove away. I turned to the sign and stared at it, trying to find some sort of explanation in it, but I couldn't. There was no explanation, no answers. All I knew was Leah was gone. I was completely blindsided. In an instant, I went from worrying something might have happened to her or at the very least that she was working herself into oblivion to regain ground after the failed retreat, to facing the reality that she was simply gone.

Realizing I'd left my phone inside, I went in and called

her. I didn't expect her to actually answer. But I did expect her voicemail. At least then I could have left her a message. Instead, I got a monotonous voice telling me the number I'd dialed was disconnected. It wasn't just that Leah was no longer physically present, that she wasn't in her house anymore. She was no longer a part of my life at all.

I loved her. I knew that with every bit of me. And I believed she loved me too. I'd convinced myself I was as important to her as she was to me, and that we had something special. Every day since finding out about the tour, I'd been thinking about how we were going to make it work. I'd spent hours poring over the schedule and figuring out how to get her from here to various places so we could spend even just a day together. It was supposed to be a big surprise for her, and I'd even started getting excited about what it was going to be like to travel around and experience this with her.

Now that was gone along with Leah. All my images of what our future could be and how our relationship would continue to build, and grow were snatched away from me. I loved her, but I was wrong about her loving me. The pain was instant and intense, and I knew it wouldn't go away anytime soon. I had to throw myself into thinking about something else to stop myself from going crazy.

For the next few days, I was still somewhat in denial. It just couldn't be real. There had to be some sort of misunderstanding. Something happened and there was a miscommunication between Leah and the landlord. I figured I would wake up or come home and she would be there. She would call me or text me, and I'd find out she lost her phone or broke it and that's why the number was disconnected.

But by the end of the week, when the landlord came by with a couple wanting to look at the apartment, full reality hit me hard. There was no misunderstanding or miscommunication. Leah really was gone.

I tried to focus on the upcoming tour to keep me distracted and stop the pain. But my heart was broken. Even thinking about the amazing opportunity and the benefit this tour could have on my life and the future of my career didn't help to lessen the blow. I wasn't looking forward to it anymore. I couldn't be happy about it. All I wanted was Leah. The only thing I could do was turn to writing songs to help deal with the pain. And soon I was surrounded by page after page of lyrics.

LEAH - TEN MONTHS LATER

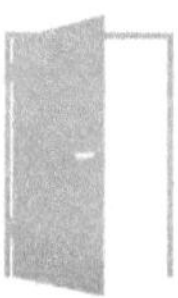

"You can always go home again."

That's what they always say, isn't it?

Of course, it was one of those things that people said with the ubiquitous "they" who no one knew and they never specified. That always got to me, and now I knew exactly why. It's because the "they" people talked about when they said those types of things didn't know shit about what they were talking about. That's why there were no names or qualifications. Just "they."

And what they said about going home again gave me the inkling they never did actually go home again. Or they never left to begin with.

Not that I hated being back in Dixon. It was my home, after all. My true home. The place where I was born and raised, and where my family still lived. It was the place I always thought of when it came to things like holidays and visits and feeling sentimental. When I sang that whole thing about being home for Christmas... that was Dixon.

But this wasn't a visit, and it definitely wasn't Christmas. This was just me being back in Dixon living with my parents and feeling like the biggest failure on the face of the Earth. So, in that way, sure, I could still go home again. But it wasn't the warm and fuzzy experience "they" would want you to think. Instead, I felt more like I'd dragged myself back with my tail between my legs and hoped my mother and father didn't just toss me aside.

It would have gone along with the general theme of how my life was unfolding at that point, though. I moved out of my apartment in the middle of the night like I was running from the law, paying my landlord early so he didn't throw a fit about the broken lease. That wasn't nearly as hard as quitting the job I loved. I'd worked so hard for that job and for the promotion I wouldn't have a chance to earn. I loved the job and I loved the people I worked with, but that was the very reason I had to walk away from it when I did. Piper already knew about the baby, and it wouldn't be long before everyone else I worked with found out as well. If I stayed much longer, someone would let something slip and Jayson would find out about the baby.

That wasn't something I could let happen. I made the choice not to tell him, and that was a choice I wouldn't change. He had a different life ahead of him, and I couldn't take that away from him. But I also couldn't raise the baby alone. My career was fulfilling and I enjoyed it, but my salary definitely wasn't enough to support both of us. Not with the exorbitant prices of LA. I needed to go somewhere with a lower cost of living where I could find a job that would take care of us comfortably. And I needed someone who could watch the baby while I was working, someone who would love her and ensure she was safe and had what she needed when I wasn't there to give it to her.

Which led me to the one real choice I had: I came home so my parents could help. And as demoralizing as it was, it turned out to be the best decision for me at the time. My mother was there for me throughout my pregnancy and had been a huge help since my daughter was born. Never once had she said anything to make me feel bad about what happened or to question my decisions. It was turning out in the best way it possibly could, I guessed, but it wasn't completely smooth. Being back home in the tiny town after the bright lights of the big city was a hard feeling to cope with. But at least I had my baby girl. She brought her own bright light into my life.

At the end of a long day, it was good to be back home, sitting on the couch with my baby in my arms. Breast-feeding her gave me a sense of purpose and contentment I didn't realize I could experience, and after the initial challenges, it became one of my favorite parts of taking care of her. Sitting there with her as she happily ate, I turned on the local news. In a town like Dixon, the local news didn't tend to be the most exciting thing to watch. Little happened in Dixon, and when there was something to show up on the news, it was usually no more thrilling than a house fire or a local bake sale.

That night, though, the anchor had widened eyes and seemed excited to actually have something to talk about.

"Calling all music fans. In two weeks, the national tour of The Monsters will make its way through our area. There are still tickets available, and the show promises to be..."

The rest of her overly enthusiastic presentation and canned laughter about the band name melted away in the buzzing in my ears. My jaw hung open as I stared at the screen and the images of a recent show. I knew that name. It wasn't exactly my type of music, but I knew I'd heard of the band before. That was the band Jayson was opening for during the tour. That meant he was going to be in my vicinity soon.

I sat there on the couch thinking about what that meant, trying to wrap my head around the idea of him being so close by in just two weeks. In the ten months since I'd left LA, I hadn't seen or spoken to Jayson. I knew he had called me several times. I'd listened to the messages he sent me before disconnecting my phone. It was too hard to keep ignoring him, to pretend I didn't want to pick up and talk to him. Moving back here to Dixon made me feel like I was a world away from him. There was no way I would run into him or accidentally cross paths with him.

Now it was like the universe was leading him back in my direction. Perhaps that was a bit dramatic, but I couldn't just ignore it. The news anchor said there were still tickets left for the show. If I was going to go along with the idea of all this being a sign, there being tickets left was just another one. I happened to know most of the shows in the tour sold out weeks, sometimes even months, in advance. This was too good an opportunity to pass up.

Supporting my daughter with one arm, I took out my phone with the other hand and searched the ticket sales website. Several options popped up, and I couldn't help myself. I bought a ticket and tossed my phone away as if I could somehow convince myself it was no big deal. And it really wasn't. I was just satisfying curiosity, continuing the support and encouragement I used to give the band before leaving. It wasn't like Jayson was going to see me. The concert was being held in a huge arena. It wasn't like the shows I used to go to where he would be able to look out of the crowd and see my face. There would be no winking at me or waving from behind his drums. I would just disappear into the crowd, become one of the sea of faces, and he would never even know I was there. Besides, the show was still two weeks away. I could change my mind and not go if I wanted to.

But I didn't. I woke up the morning of the show with butterflies in my stomach. I was excited to go and looking forward to hearing the band again. After ten months I was sure they had gotten even better and maybe would even have new songs for me to hear. It would be a nice little trip down memory lane, then I could go right back to the regularly scheduled program of my life and no one would know the difference.

Only, it didn't work out quite that way, either.

The show was every bit as thrilling as I thought it would be. Seeing Jayson up on the stage made my throat tighten with emotion and tugged on my heart, but it was also good. He was in his element up there. This was a much larger stage and a much bigger show than I'd ever seen him in, and it looked good on him. He looked out over the crowd and never once did his eyes settle on me. I felt guarded by the anonymity of the audience, and when the set was over, I was ready to go. Being away from the baby was difficult when it wasn't for work, and my breasts were telling me they were full and ready to be pumped. I needed to fill bottles for her for the morning so they'd be ready while I was at work.

The headlining band didn't matter to me, anyway. I was only there to see Jayson. Slipping out while the headliner was getting ready to go on meant I wouldn't have to grapple with the crowds and would get home much faster. And it would have worked if I hadn't chosen the exit I did.

I could have gone to any of the other exits in the arena. But a last-minute detour through the restroom put me at the door toward the back. I decided to leave through there and just walk around to my car rather than crossing back through the building. As I was headed to the door, I noticed a familiar figure ahead of me. Leaned against a wall, chugging from a flask, was Carter.

Shit.

I tried to turn and duck out of the way, hoping he didn't see me, but it didn't work. Before I could even change direction, he looked over at me and I saw his eyes go wide. Tucking his flask away, he rushed over toward me.

No, no, no. I couldn't get away, so I stopped and gave the guitarist a tight smile.

"Hi, Carter," I said.

He looked me up and down like he wasn't completely convinced he was seeing what he thought he was.

"Leah," he said. "I can't believe it. What are you doing here?"

I looked around and threw my arms out to the sides in a casual gesture.

"What everybody else here is doing. You know, just catching the show. You were great, by the way. You guys sound fantastic. But now I've got to be going," I said.

I started to walk around him, but Carter moved in my way to stop me.

"Jayson has been a totally fucked-up mess since you left. You ruined him. How could you do that to him, then show up here?" he asked.

The confrontation hit me in the gut and made heat crawl up the back of my neck, but I couldn't engage in it. I needed to get out of the situation and not deal with any of this anymore. This was a mistake.

"I'm sorry," I said. "And tell him I'm sorry too."

I tried to move around him again, but Carter reached out and grabbed onto my arm, stopping me.

"Oh, no. You're not getting off that easy. You're not just going to tell me to tell Jayson you're sorry and then disappear again. You pulled that shit once. It's not happening this time. I'm bringing you into Jayson so you can answer for yourself," Carter said.

He started to drag me down the corridor toward what I was assuming was the door to the band's green room. In a moment of panic, I kicked out and caught Carter right in the shin. He grimaced and let go of me. The distraction was just enough for me to slip away and run to the parking lot. I didn't stop until I got to my car and took off. I was afraid to see Jayson, worried about what Carter would tell him.

It was stupid of me to go to the concert. I should have stayed home. I felt like such an idiot.

JAYSON

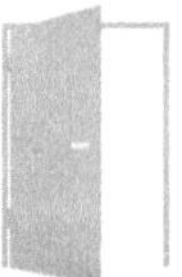

Even after being on tour for so many months, finishing up a set and listening to the audience roar and cheer was a special kind of high. It started building even before we walked out on stage and kept getting stronger as we played. It was our job to warm up the crowd, to get them going so they were ready for The Monsters. We did our job well. We walked out on stage to an audience that was feeling edgy, cold, and anxious. They wanted the show. They wanted to lose themselves in the music and have fun. So we whipped them up and got them having fun before the headliners came in for the main event.

The whole process sent a rush of adrenaline through me. These days, it was the closest thing I had to feeling happy. Any sense of real happiness was a thing of the past, but at least when I was up on stage and heard people cheering and singing, I felt like I could get out of myself and focus on something else. This tour was the only thing I had going for me in life, so I wanted to give everything to it. I poured myself out to every show and tried to make the experience as good as possible for the people who filled the seats.

That was why even after our set was over and the headlining band took the stage, I didn't head immediately into the green room the way the rest of the band did. They wanted to kick back and relax, and even take advantage of the spoils of the tour. That changed somewhat depending on our location, but it usually consisted of food, alcohol, and women. There was always an abundance of all of them, offered up to us to enjoy after our shows. The other guys, particularly Mark and Carter, took advantage of these offerings as much as they possibly could. But not me. As soon as we finished playing, I went backstage and put myself in the prime position to watch the rest of the show.

Having the vantage point of being backstage didn't just give me the opportunity to listen to the music and enjoy the performance in front of me. I saw it as a learning opportunity, the chance to elevate my performance quality at every show. There was a reason The Monsters were already popular, and their popularity was growing with every show. I wanted the type of star quality they had and the ability to fill arenas like they did. That meant watching their performances and trying to pick up hints on how to improve how I played, how I interacted with the audience, and anything else I could discover.

It was working. I could already tell a difference between the way I performed at the beginning of the tour and now. The third song of the headlining set was just getting good when I felt someone come up behind me. I looked to my side and saw Carter. There was something urgent in his eyes, and he leaned close to my ear to talk to me.

"I need to tell you something," he said.

"After the show," I told him.

Carter shook his head. "Now. It's important. Back to the green room where it's quieter."

Even in the loud sound of the backstage, I could tell there was something serious in his voice, so I nodded. I followed him to the green room and immediately noticed the small swarm of women Mark had assembled. He hadn't taken much time that night. It was almost impressive if it hadn't also been somewhat depressing.

"All right. All of you out," Carter instructed. "Thank you for visiting. Feel free to wait outside the building. Tickets may be available to future shows. Come see us again."

He stood by the door, gesturing like he was trying to sweep the women out of the room.

"Hey!" Mark shouted from the couch where he was sitting with his arms around two women. "What the hell?"

"You heard me. They need to go," Carter said. "They are welcome to come do the Roman orgy thing some other time, but for right now, I need them gone."

The women stood and threw Carter nasty looks as they sashayed out of the room. Mark jumped to his feet and approached Carter angrily.

"What the hell do you think you're doing? This isn't just your room, you know. And those women came here to see me."

Carter shook his head incredulously, then opened the door he had just closed.

"You know what, Mark? You're right. They were kind enough to follow you in here. The least you can do is go with them," he said.

Out of the corner of my eye, I saw Luke hide a laugh as Carter shoved Mark out of the room and closed the door behind him. For a second I was sure Mark was going to burst back in and we'd have a brawl on our hands, but the door stayed shut and Carter came farther into the room.

"What is this all about?" I asked.

Carter paced back and forth across the room for a second like he was trying to build himself up to tell me something. Finally, he took a step closer to me.

"All right. Listen. After the set, I went out in the hall. Mark was already building up his harem in here, and I didn't feel like dealing with that shit right now. So I went out there to cool off a bit," he said.

"Probably chugging down some booze to lower your body temperature," Luke interjected with a laugh.

"Shut up," Carter snapped. "I don't see you leading the temperance parade, either."

Luke looked at the bottle of beer in his hand, shrugged, and took another swig of it. I could see this conversation was already going off the rails. If I had any chance of getting back into the wing to listen to the rest of the set, I needed to help it along.

"Okay, so you were in the hall. So, what? Why did you need to bring me back here to tell me that?" I asked.

"It's not that I was *in* the hall. It's what I saw in the hall," he said. "I was just standing there, and I looked up and saw this woman coming toward the exit. At first, I didn't think anything of it. I figured she was lost trying to find her way out or something, but then I realized her face looked familiar."

"Who was it?" I asked.

"It took me a second, but then it hit me. I did know her. It was that girl you used to hang out with. Leah," Carter said.

Bright flashes of color burst in front of my eyes, and I

felt like the world was spinning around me. Heat burned on my neck and face, and it was like someone had punched a hole in the center of my chest. I blinked a few times, trying to process what he just said.

"Leah?" I asked. "You saw Leah?"

"Yep," Carter said with a nod."

"You're telling me Leah is here? At the arena? She came to see the show?" I asked.

"She was definitely here, and she said she watched the show. As a matter of fact, she said we sounded great."

I launched at Carter, grabbing him by the front of his shirt so he had to look at me.

"You have to bring me to her. Did you see where she was headed? Did she mention where her seats were? I need you to bring me to her," I said again.

Carter shook his head.

"I can't. She's long gone."

"What do you mean she's long gone?"

Carter pulled free and brushed his hand down the front of his shirt like he was trying it to get rid of the feeling of me holding on to him.

"I tried to bring her back here to talk to you. I told her how messed up it was what she did to you and said she needed to come back here and talk to you about it. But she took off running toward the parking lot."

"Fuck," I muttered and dropped down onto the couch.

I covered my face and let out a groan of despair. How could this even happen? It had been so long. Ten months without a single word from her. The day she disappeared from my bed was it between us. I never saw her or heard from her again. Finally heading out on the tour with the band was my only saving grace, the thing that kept me distracted and prevented me from driving myself completely crazy at home without her.

Now she was suddenly resurfacing? After all this time, she was here? At one of my shows?

"I can't believe I fucking missed her," I said. "She was right here, at my fucking show, and I didn't see her."

"At least she was here," Carter pointed out, trying to comfort me.

It didn't have exactly the reassuring effect he wanted it to, but it did make me think.

"You know what? You're right. She was here."

"Yeah, I know," he said, sounding slightly confused. "That's what I just said."

"No, I mean, she was here." I pointed down at the floor. "Not just at a show, but at *this* show. I highly doubt she just randomly decided to travel some far distance to see us play. That means she has to live around this area, right?"

"I guess that makes sense," Carter said. "She did rush out of here pretty fast and didn't want to see any of us. I'd think if she made a trip to see the show, she'd at least want to hang out and say hi afterward. It must have just been close by and easy for her to get here."

"Exactly," I said.

I pulled out my old, battered laptop and started searching. I wasn't sure what I was searching for, but I dug and dug, following every lead I could think of. It took me all the way through the concert, and the lead singer of The Monsters poked his head into the room.

"Hey guys. Great show. We're going to go hit up some of the local bars. Want to come?" he asked.

Carter and Luke immediately agreed, but I shook my head.

"Thanks for the offer, but I can't," I told him, then

looked at Carter. "You guys go ahead. I'm just going to pack up and go back to the hotel to keep doing this."

"You sure?" Carter asked. "I could stay with you."

"No. It's fine. You go blow off some steam and have fun."

I kept searching through the night until I couldn't stay awake any longer. When I woke up, I went right back to the search. I narrowed it down further and further until I stumbled on an old county phone book. I looked up her last name and found only one entry. Hoping it was the right address, I jotted it down and put it through my GPS. She was nearby.

The other guys were still asleep, so I slipped out of the hotel without waking them up. I hopped into the rental car we got to help us get around during this most recent cluster of shows and headed out. By nine that morning, I was pulling up to a small, well-kept house in a rural town.

LEAH

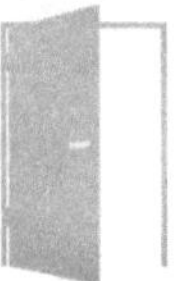

I didn't know of anywhere else in the world where the paperboy knocked on every door to deliver the paper rather than just tossing it onto the front porch in the morning. But that's the way it was in Dixon. Sometimes on the weekdays, he would go old-school and we'd start the day with the sound of the paper thudding into the middle of the door or dropping onto the sidewalk. Not on Sundays. Every week when the time to deliver the Sunday paper rolled around, Steven would walk around going door to door. He greeted each family by name and handed them their paper. It was a nice touch that I was sure earned him a lot of tips. At least one, I knew for a fact, since I was the one to give it to him.

So, when I heard the knock on the door Sunday morning, I wasn't surprised. It was later than usual, but at least he was there and I'd have the paper for coupons for the week. I went for my purse and grabbed out his usual tip, then opened the door without bothering to check through the window. But it wasn't Steven standing on the doorstep with his big smile and a newspaper in his hand.

It was Jayson.

I couldn't believe what I was seeing. Stunned by finding him outside my door, I just stood there, gripping the money and staring at him. There was really nothing else I could do. My brain had gone blank the moment I laid eyes on him, and I no longer had the ability to process cohesive thought much less put together enough of a logical progression to do anything. He looked back at me, finally cocking his head slightly to the side before he spoke.

"Hello, Leah," he said.

Just like that. After all this time and him showing up unannounced on my porch, that was all he could come up with. "Hello, Leah." But at least the words startled my brain back into functioning and the thoughts started flowing again.

What was he doing there? How did he even find me? What the fuck was I supposed to do now?

"Leah? Can I come inside?" Jayson asked.

I didn't really have a choice. He was standing right there in front of me. This wasn't a phone call I could push off or a text I could just not answer and hope it disappeared after a while. Jayson was on my front porch and wanted to come in to talk to me. This wasn't a moment I'd ever planned on happening. Not a moment I ever wanted to happen. But it was happening now, and there wasn't anything I could do about it. I just had to deal with it as it came.

And be extremely thankful my parents had already left for church. I didn't need to get them involved in this too. Not yet. I took a deep breath and opened the door more. I reluctantly stepped out of the way and gestured for him to come inside. Jayson stepped past me, and I shut the door behind him. That brought me to the end of the list of things I could think of to do in the situation, and I stood with my back against the door, staring at him. I wondered what the chances were he would just have a few words to say to me, then leave and go about his life satisfied with the closure.

I was thinking the chances weren't good.

"Carter told me you were at the show last night," he said.

Now I knew the chances weren't good. I wasn't going to be able to get him out of the house fast enough for everything to fall back into place the way it had been. Everything had been carrying on just as I'd intended it to for the last ten months. But there was no way that was going to continue now.

"I was," I told him. "A couple weeks ago the news had a bit about the tour coming this way, so I got a ticket."

He stared at me for a second, then shook his head slightly, his eyes narrowing. "Why didn't you try to see me?"

"I thought it would be too hard," I admitted.

That wasn't exactly the way I intended to say it, but at that point there was no reason to keep trying to hide it. Jayson looked at me, the weight of his gaze on me heavy. There was so much behind his eyes, and I could feel it pressing down on me.

"Why did you leave without saying a word?" he asked.

I swallowed, trying to force down the emotion that was building up in my throat and aching through my jaw.

"At the last show I went to, Luke told Piper about the band going on tour. You hadn't said anything to me about it, and I figured that meant you might be conflicted about the whole thing, so I helped you with the decision," I told him.

"What are you talking about?" he asked. "What decision?"

"About us. You needed to go on the tour. It was a great opportunity. And I wasn't going to stand in the way of that. But you are the kind of guy who would think twice about it. I didn't want you to have to, so I made the decision for you," I explained.

"I could have done both. I could have gone on the road and continued our relationship. I hadn't told you about the tour yet because I was trying to get all the plans into place for all the times we would be able to see each other while I was on the road. We could have stayed together and just had a long-distance relationship while I was touring," he said.

I shook my head, closing my eyes briefly to stop the words from sinking in too deep.

"You don't understand," I told him. "You just don't understand."

Jayson took a step closer to me and grabbed me by my upper arms.

"What don't I understand? I don't understand that I can't stand being away from you? I don't understand that I'm in love with you? That I need you? That I'd give anything and do anything to have you back?"

It was all so overwhelming, so much that I couldn't get my mind to wrap around it. I could barely breathe. I couldn't process what he was saying or how I was supposed to respond. I never intended on telling him what was going on, but even if I was ever was going to, this definitely wasn't the way it was supposed to play out.

Then in that moment, the option got taken away from me. Just like I'd helped Jayson make the decision about the continuation of our future, my baby girl helped me make the decision about what I was going to tell Jayson. His eyes widened when he heard her start to cry. A long breath escaped my lungs. This was it. There was no point in trying to avoid it now. I took his hand and guided him through the house to my bedroom. A little white crib set up against the wall made up the nursery, and inside it, my daughter was fussing. Our daughter.

I released Jayson's hand and went to the side of the crib. Reaching in gently, I scooped the baby out and into my arms. She settled down as I cradled her close to my chest and turned back to face Jayson.

"This is what you don't understand," I told him. "I found out I was pregnant not long before I found out about the tour. I hadn't figured out the perfect time to tell you yet, and then when I heard Luke talking about the tour, I knew I couldn't tell you. Would you have really left on tour for a year if you knew I was having your baby?"

He looked completely shocked, but I couldn't decipher the range of the emotions he was feeling. His expression was pure surprise, and he stayed completely silent for several long seconds, just staring at the baby in my arms. Finally, he stepped up closer and held his arms out toward me.

"Can I hold her?" he asked.

Emotion leapt inside me, and I nodded. Gently transferring our baby into Jayson's arms, I took a step back and let him cradle his daughter. He was so careful, so loving, my heart melted. The way he gazed down at her was everything I'd always wanted to see in his face but never allowed myself to hope for.

"What's her name?" he asked.

"Harper Grace," I told him.

He looked down at her and the tenderness on his face was enough to weaken my knees.

"I wanted you to have your dream," I explained. "You had worked so hard to get there, and it was finally happening for you. We were in such a good place, and I thought there could one day be a future for us, but a baby wasn't in the plans for right then. We never even talked about how you felt about children or if you wanted any. I decided I wanted you to follow your dream, and I wasn't going to stand in your way."

Jayson looked up at me from staring down into Harper's face.

"That might have been my dream, but now I have a new dream. I want a family. With you. I want to be a father to our baby," he told me.

Harper's eyes drifted closed, and she fell comfortably back to sleep. Jayson carried her over to the crib and gently settled her back down. I took him by his hand and guided him out of the room, closing the door behind us. I walked him back into the living room before turning to him.

"I don't see how things could work, Jayson. You're on the road. I have a tiny baby," I pointed out.

"*We* have a tiny baby," he corrected. "I'm going to do everything in my power to make this work."

His eyes stayed locked on mine for another second before he leaned forward and kissed me. The instant his mouth touched mine, sparks flew.

The kiss was long and insistent, pressing months of being away from each other and the thousands of kisses that should have been into one passionate embrace. His tongue slipped inside, and mine met it. I leaned back on the couch, and he followed me down, hovering over me as his hand slid down my side. I wrapped my leg around him and could feel the bulge in his pants as his weight pressed down into me. The smell of his skin was intoxicating, and I buried my face in his chest, pressing my lips into him as if I could take back the days with each one.

One hand found my jeans button and flipped it open, and his strong, sure hands clasped at the waistband. There was no hesitation and no hurry, but a controlled sense of assurance. This was what was meant to be. I lifted my backside so he could pull the pants off me, and they soon found themselves flung across the floor. The black, lacy panties I wore underneath seemed to mesmerize him, and I bit my bottom lip as I watched the obvious desire cross his face.

Half standing, with one knee still on the couch between my legs, he unbuttoned his shirt quickly, pulling it off to reveal his chiseled muscles bungling out of his white, cotton T-shirt underneath. I sat up to stop his hands working on his belt. That was something I wanted to have the privilege of. His mouth crushed into mine for another kiss as I unbuckled his belt and grasped blindly at his zipper, pulling it down and reaching my hand inside. His warm, thick cock pressed against the fabric of his pants, and I stroked it over the boxers. Jayson let out an audible moan, and his fingers began working on the buttons of my blouse. When they were undone, he flicked the snap in the center of my bra expertly and the tension released.

Reluctantly, I took my hand out of his pants and removed the blouse, pausing to let his eyes roam my body while I removed the bra. Tossing it to the ground, I watched as he licked his top lip at the sight of my breasts and stood fully to remove his pants. I waited in anticipation as he pulled at the waistband of his boxers, letting his cock spring out. I sat back up again, not waiting for him to sit, and clasped my hand over the base, stroking it as his hands slid down my chest to cup my breasts. His fingers played with my nipples as our mouths reached for one another again, tongues desperate for the taste of the other. A long, tense kiss was broken when he unfolded himself back up again, and I took the opportunity to run my lips across his chest. I licked the muscles on his stomach as I worked my way down, stroking him slowly as I went along, until finally I reached the base of his cock and looked up into his eyes.

JAYSON

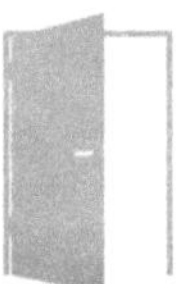

Her large, almond-shaped eyes stared up at me as she stroked me, the head of my cock brushing against the side of her face. The intensity of the moment was building even still, and the anticipation of her warm, wet lips wrapping around my cock was almost too much to bear. A wide smile crossed her lips, and her tongue flicked out to run across the length of me, sending shudders down my spine and lighting all my senses. She continued to stroke me as her tongue made its way all around me, wetting me and making her long, confident strokes all the more intense. She placed her lips at the head and slowly took me into her, and I barely kept my knees locked as the sensation of her lips wrapped around me eclipsed all other thoughts.

She stroked me as she took me into her mouth, and the sensation was so strong I felt like I could have come immediately if I didn't slow down. It had been months since I had been able to pleasure her body, and I wanted the time to do so first. But she was insistent, as hungry to please me as I was to please her. Her head bobbed on me, and one hand slipped under to cradle and gently massage my balls. Then she moved her mouth down, continuing to stroke me, as she took them into her lips one by one, nearly sending me spiraling into a climax.

I couldn't stand there any longer. Gently pushing her back, I knelt down onto the floor and pulled her by a willing hand to join me. Our lips met again as she lay on the floor, and I positioned myself on top of her. My cock teased at her core, and I fought off the desire to plunge into her right then. Instead, I moved my kisses to her neck and down to her collarbone. I slid my tongue across her chest and made a trail down the center, then blew a stream of hot breath over the wet line, reveling in the shiver it sent up her.

Moving farther down, I traced the areola of one breast with my tongue and then slid my tongue over it in a long, slow movement. My hand followed the motion on the other breast as I flicked the nipple with my tongue and let my other hand slide down her center. I wanted to stimulate her as much as possible, to envelop her with my touch so much that the months that we missed would disappear in a haze of pleasure. My roaming hand reached her hot, wet core, and I brought it back up to lick the pad of my thumb before bringing it down again.

With my mouth on one nipple, one hand massaging the other breast, my free hand pulled aside her panties and the thumb pressed down into her folds, circling in slow movements and eliciting a cry of pleasure from Leah. She wiggled under my touch, but I began to press down on her pearl in the center, and her legs wrapped around me as she arched her back. Suddenly, I thrust forward and plunged into her, my thumb still circling her clit and my mouth taking her nipple in to suckle. She let out a yelp that filled me with an intense desire to feel her orgasm around me. I rocked back and thrust again, increasing the speed of my thumb and clenching her full, heaving breast in my other hand.

I was completely immersed in her pleasure, and I filled her and titillated her as much as I could. Her hips wiggled and writhed below me, and I knew she was about to tumble into a powerful climax. Pressing down on her center, I thrust deeply into her, pushing against the back of her walls until I felt her release and her legs vibrate around me as they clenched on and off around my hips. Her voice rose to a near scream as the orgasm took control of her, and her arms wrapped around my neck.

"Please," she whispered in my ear, pleading with me to give her what we were both denied for so long. The mere request, the desperation and begging tone in her voice, was enough to send me into overdrive. No longer would I be holding back. I rose up, pulling her legs over so they lay together and her body was turned sideways. She still faced up toward me, and I relished in the view of her perfect breasts as they bounced while I slammed into her with a rhythmic pounding that satisfied the frustration and loneliness of the past few months. It washed away with every rock back and forth, and I let myself disappear into the cathartic release of her body accepting mine, letting me dominate her in this way before we wrapped back up together and stayed that way until life made us part.

I clenched at her hips to pull her closer and sank as deeply in her as I could go. As I pulled back, she moved her legs and I pulled her to me, picking her up and then lying back so she straddled me. I clenched her close to me so that while she was on top, I still controlled the movements. I arched up and thrust into her from below, and the delighted cries from Leah were muffled as her lips pursed against my neck and chest. I knew my control was being lost, and soon I would have nothing left to stop me from spiraling into a climax of my own, so I tried to slow down, and Leah took the opportunity to begin her own motion on top of me.

I lay back and watched with wonder as she placed her hands on my chest and arched up. Her breasts bounced playfully as she rode me, and her head fell back, her eyes closed as she concentrated on the feeling of her walls stretching to accommodate me in this position. She slowed the rhythm down, and soon it was measured and patient. But while it was slower, the intensity was building again. Our eyes locked on one another as she reached back with one hand to massage me while she rode. I reached up to fill my hands with her breasts and pressed them into her, kneading them. With her free hand, she took one of my fingers and placed it on her lips. As she slowly sank down onto me, she took it into her mouth, simulating the motion of her body on mine.

Our bodies were one unit, working together to pleasure each other at the highest levels. My finger sank deep into her mouth as she sat down fully on my throbbing cock, and I knew that I was going to come soon. She seemed to see it in my eyes, and her rhythm increased, her hips rocking and her clit brushing against my center. I took the now wet fingers and traced them down her center until they reached her core and pressed them into place. She responded by clutching my wrist, guiding my fingers to the motion she needed from me as she began to bounce on me. Within moments, her cries filled the room and she clenched, falling into another powerful orgasm. As her body regained control, she pulled at my neck and I sat up, picking her up in one motion without leaving her and placing her back on the couch.

Our hands locked into one another, and I pulled them over her head. Her legs wrapped around me, squeezing as if she were willing me to push as deeply as I could. She bit her top lip, and our eyes met again, and I could see the desire for me to take her hard in them. She wanted me to climax as she had, and I knew I couldn't hold on any longer as it was. I began to slam into her again, slowly at first, but when her voice yelped out in pleasure, it arose a need in me. I slid my hands to her wrists and held them down into the couch as my cock dove into her over and over, and I began to lose control. I clasped for her lips with my own, and our tongues twisted and danced with each other as her legs squeezed around my hips. I sank deeply into her and exploded, a climax more powerful than any other in my entire life completely overtaking me as I came and roared out. My voice echoed and died as my body twitched, and I filled her, emptying myself completely and collapsing into her waiting arms.

Her breasts engulfed me as I laid my face between them and listened to her heartbeat, so rapid and intense at first, and then slowing as our bodies calmed.

I didn't want to let her go. I held on to Leah as tightly as I could, wanting to keep the moment going. Having her in my arms again was everything I'd been needing those past long months. Ten months was already a long time. Being away from her made it feel that much longer. Touring was absolutely grueling, and there were moments when I felt so overwhelmed and alone. Those were the moments when not having Leah there with me were the worst.

I missed her all the time. When I was excited about a particularly good show, I wanted to share it with her. When there was the rare funny moment, I wanted her there to experience it with me. But it was the times when I was exhausted after playing show after show and barely getting any sleep, or when I was the only one who stayed in rather than going out to bars or after-hours clubs with the other band members, those were the times when I felt her absence the most. I miss having her there to listen to me, to comfort me and make me feel whole.

I couldn't live without her. That was more obvious than ever. Especially now that I knew living without her would be living without our daughter. That just wasn't an option. But that left me with not knowing what to do next. I knew I couldn't ask her to come on the road and bring along our infant child. That would be too much for both of them. All I could do right then was hold her close and hope I would figure out the right answer.

Leah snuggled closer, her head on my chest and her arm draped over my waist.

"What happens now?" she asked.

I kissed her head and rested my head against it.

"Well, the tour is almost finished, and the band will be heading back to Los Angeles. We don't know what's going to happen after that, but I want you to come back to LA with me," I told her.

"Go back with you?" she asked, sounding surprised by the suggestion.

"Of course. We can move into a bigger place together. Be a family."

She sighed and snuggled closer. "Having a family isn't exactly conducive to getting a music career off the ground," she pointed out.

"I know my career isn't ideal. But I'm willing to work as hard as I have to in order to be a good partner for you and a good father to our daughter. I promise you no matter what it takes, you and Harper will always come first. Even if that means having to give up music and get a suit-and-tie-type job so it's easier for us to be together," I vowed.

She shook her head and laughed. "I hope it won't come to that."

"I hope it won't either," he agreed. "Because I'm really only good at beating on things, and ties make me feel like I'm being slowly strangled."

She laughed again. "What am I going to do with you?"

I took her by her arms and adjusted her position so she was above me, looking down into my face.

"You're going to love me," I told her. "Forever."

She smiled and kissed me.

"Yes, I am."

EPILOGUE

LEAH - ONE YEAR LATER

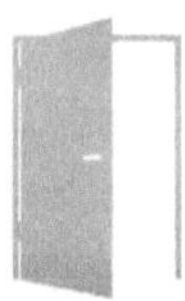

"Do you think that picture makes my nose look big?" Jayson asked.

I wished he had waited for at least a few seconds, because right at the moment he was asking, I was taking a long sip out of my glass of iced tea. It took all my control to hold back my full laugh until I swallowed so I could keep the tea in my mouth. Even though I knew he was joking, I couldn't help but look out the window beside me at the billboard.

It was amazing how much could change in just one year. Only a year ago I was in Dixon, still trying to get my bearings as a single mother and figure out what life ahead of me was going to look like. I thought I'd lost the love of my life forever and was going to have to sit back and watch while Jayson thrived and found a new life without ever knowing what ours could have been.

Now I was sitting in a restaurant in Hollywood, looking out a window at a massive billboard with Jayson's face on it.

The rest of the band was on it too, but his face was front and center. And it certainly did make him look big.

"Yes," I told him. "It really does."

The billboard had just gone up two days before, and we were both getting used to it. There was something simultaneously jarring and exciting about looking up and seeing my partner twenty feet tall in the middle of a billboard. The board was to advertise the band's new album, and it was already getting tons of press. The first album was good and brought a lot of attention, but this one was shattering that success. The band had finally broken through and was bigger than ever. Bigger than any of them had ever dared dream of being. The tour with The Monsters had been their springboard, and it had only been an upward climb since then.

Things were happening fast. Every day it seemed they were getting more popular and the world wanted a little bit more of them. Talk shows had started calling for interviews, and every week they got more invitations to play gigs with huge exposure. They had even gotten to the point where they were having to turn down performances and could negotiate higher prices because they were in such high demand, they were getting double or even triple booked for some weekends.

It didn't surprise me, but it was still stunning to watch. From the very beginning, I'd believed in them. I always knew they could hit the big time, but now that it was happening, it was awe-inspiring.

A waitress walked up to the table looking down at the pad in her hand. Without even glancing up at us, she rattled off a greeting and then the list of specials for the day. It was only after she had gotten through the entree options and was moving on to desserts that she bothered to lift her eyes.

They swept over me with barely a notice, but when they hit Jayson, her gaze stopped.

I watched her eyes widen and the color first drain from her face, the rush back into it to create a bright red glow across her cheeks. She started stuttering, babbling incoherently about who Jayson was and what he might like to eat. Finally, she stopped and took a breath.

"Can I get a selfie with you?" she asked.

He nodded. "Sure."

The young waitress scrambled to get her phone out as fast as she could as Jayson stood and positioned himself beside her. She leaned her head near his and smiled broadly, snapping one picture before slightly adjusting her position and snapping another. She started to turn and kiss him on the cheek, but Jayson was already very familiar with that maneuver. He deftly moved out of the way to avoid the kiss without hurting the waitress's feelings. She thanked him and stuffed her phone back in the pocket of her apron, scurrying away into the kitchen. Jayson laughed and shook his head.

"She didn't take our order," I pointed out.

He laughed again. "No, she didn't."

It didn't bother me. There might have been a point in my life when it would have gotten to me watching a bunch of other women flirt with the guy I was dating. But I didn't feel that way with Jayson. I realized this type of attention and silly moments like that with the waitress were just the start of women falling all over themselves to get close to him. It didn't intimidate me or even make me uncomfortable. In the end, they were trying to get close to my man, and we both took that distinction very seriously. I was completely confident in my relationship with him and the way he felt about me. So, instead of feeling jealous, I felt proud. My man was a rock god, not to mention sexy as hell. But he was also faithful. I trusted him fully, and that felt good.

Beside me, Harper started fussing in her highchair. She was getting so big. It felt like just a few days ago I was cradling her in my arms as a newborn, and now she was taking shaky steps and babbling nonstop. I was sure she'd be talking way before she turned two. She was so much of a little person already, and I saw her daddy in her more and more every day. They had gotten extraordinarily close, and I loved to watch their relationship, even if it did occasionally make me feel like I was on the outside. It was definitely something I was willing to be on the outside of.

Jayson leaned close to her and took her hands, bouncing them playfully. He started signing her the little song he had written for her when she was just a few months old, and it instantly soothed her. She cooed and giggled along with him, and I could have sworn I heard her humming along at the right tune. She was going to be a musician like him one day. Maybe not playing the drums. Hopefully not playing the drums. I didn't think I could handle two people practicing the drums in the house at the same time. But she had music in her, and one day it would become something amazing.

He finished his song and kissed Harper on the tip of her nose. I loved how good he was with her and felt a familiar surge of gratitude. Things could have been so different. He could have never come to find me. He could have never wanted anything to do with me. He could have found out about our daughter and withdrawn, not wanting to be a father. They were all possibilities, and I felt so lucky that none of them happened. Instead, I got an incredible man and an incredible father for my daughter.

A few moments later, the waitress returned to the table with a sheepish expression on her face.

"Are you ready to order?" she asked, obviously embarrassed by her oversight and hoping she could just gloss right over it and we wouldn't notice.

Jayson and I ordered, and the waitress disappeared again. When she was gone, Jayson turned his attention back to me.

"There's something I wanted to talk to you about," he said.

"All right. Go ahead," I said.

"It's time for the band to go on tour again. But this time, you're coming with us," he announced.

"Oh, I am?" I asked.

He gave a single sharp nod as if it were a forgone conclusion.

"Yes. As our manager."

I laughed. "What kind of craziness are you talking now?"

"Luke has been trying to manage us alongside our agent, but it's really not working out now that we're as big as we are. Let's face it. You've been doing a lot of the work, not to mention doing a hell of a job tracking our expenses. So, I've talked to the guys and everyone agrees. You're the new manager."

"Just like that? No talking about it or anything?" I asked.

"Nope." He shook his head, and I laughed. "And I've managed to negotiate for a bus to be just the three of us. I know it will be hard at times, but I can't be separated from my family. Would you be willing to give being on the road with me a shot?"

I nodded. "I knew you'd be on the road when we got

together, and I expected you to be gone for stretches of time. It means a lot to me that you'd ask us to come. I don't want to be without you, and I don't want to deprive you of being able to watch your little girl grow up."

"Really? You'll come?" he asked, sounding excited.

"Yes. As long as Harper and I get some undisturbed sleep."

Jayson grinned. "I promise to make sure you do. And if I fuck up, you have my permission to call the landlord and have me evicted."

I laughed and leaned over the table to kiss him. I would live with all the noise in the world for a lifetime of those kisses.

THE END